KICKFLIP SUMMER

DANIELLE JACKS

Kara

All I want is one last summer of fun with my best friend, Toby.

Blue Oaks Theme Park seems like a perfect place to work while blowing off some steam. It's our last summer before university and we want to make every day count. The thing I didn't consider was being attracted to my new boss.

But it's just one summer. One quick fling. What harm can it do?

Bear

Returning home is something I can't avoid. My dad wants me to start getting serious about my future, while I want to spend the summer teaching kids skateboarding.

As always, he gets his own way, but when a cute brunette – literally – knocks me off my feet, I'm finding the theme park interesting in a whole new way.

A summer romance. Totally insubstantial. I can handle that. Right?

Two people brought together by chance. Both finding something they don't know they need. A sweet romance about finding a home in the heart.

Kickflip Summer is written in British English. This book is the work of fiction. Any names, characters, places, and events are either creations of the author's imagination or used fictitiously. Any similarities are purely coincidental.

Cover design: Pink Elephant Designs.

Editor: Karen Sanders.

Proofreader: Mich Feeney.

Formatter: Pink Elephant Designs.

The things you are most scared of are usually the most rewarding.

NOTE TO THE READER

This book is written in British English. The author is from England, United Kingdom. British spellings and phrases are used throughout this story. The legal age for drinking alcohol in the UK is eighteen years old. The age of consent for sexual activity is sixteen; although there is no explicit content within these pages the act is implied.

CHAPTER ONE

KARA

Kara, this is exactly what we've been looking for."

Toby slams the newspaper down in front of me, jabbing it with his finger.

My twin nieces circle the breakfast table, almost knocking the end chair over as they fly around the bend, giggling like wild hyenas. They are both too hyper for this time in the morning which my sister has already pointed out. The school holidays already have them behaving like younger children, even though they'll be going to high school in September. My gaze drifts over the page, taking in the article Toby so desperately wants me to see.

"A day at the theme park sounds fun. I'm game for an adventure."

He frames the moment with his hands, ready to pitch what I know will be a crazy idea. This is one of the things I love about my best friend. He has the gift of being able to dream up all sorts of schemes.

"Hear me out," Toby says. "Imagine a whole summer of adventure. England doesn't get much better than Blue Oaks. There are ten zones to explore, and each one offers a different setting. This could be our last opportunity before life gets real. Plus, I've already outgrown Hexham. It's a small town. Even travelling into Newcastle has lost its shine. I need something more."

I fiddle with the corner of the newspaper. "I'm pretty certain university is one big party. It's only a couple of months away and we'll be living the dream."

"Maybe for you. I intend to knuckle down and get on with my work."

"Yeah, right. Your nose will be sniffing out fun the second we arrive." I laugh.

"The good times start right here."

He pokes the newspaper again, circling the *Adventure Land* zone. The theme park is the biggest in the country and filled with all kinds of attractions.

"Blue Oaks Theme Park is looking for inspirational talents to help join their award-winning team. We could be their missing piece," Toby says.

"I doubt the candyfloss maker or ride operators have won any awards. Take this guy in the picture, for instance. His lightning bolt smile might win a beauty contest, but I don't think he has inspirational talents." I giggle at my assumption.

Toby shakes his head. "You've no imagination. We could be ghosts in the haunted house, or merry-go-round operators. I've always wanted to ride a roller-coaster after dark. Imagine late night campfire talks and golf buggy hijacks. We could slum it camping on the local site. For all you know, the guy in the picture might just be your perfect match. Mid-summer strolls and kisses under the moonlight could happen right here." He points to a picture of a big lake in the foreground of a beautiful mansion.

"I think you've been watching too many princess movies."

"Dream big or miss out. That's my motto."

My fingertips wander over the print, examining the threads of the advertisement. I find the information about our mystery guy. Shaking my head, a mixture of a snort and a laugh comes out before I can stop it.

"His name is Julian. Doesn't that say it all?"

"You're overthinking it. What's so bad about his name?"

"He's probably a player and too interested in the gel in his hair to invest his time in a girl."

"You've got it all wrong. Anything is possible. A summer fling is on the cards. You just need a leap of faith. Plus, I need a test run on how to make new friends so I'm a pro by freshers' week."

"You don't need any help making friends. You're the life and soul of any party. I'll be the one needing help making a good first impression. The only way I manage to get people to like me is if you've already given me a foot in the door. I'm the token best friend, not the leading lady."

Toby is the confident one in our friendship. I'm more of a tag along, happy to follow his lead. It's always been this way, and usually I'm happy to go with the flow. I only speak up when his crazy plans get out of hand.

"You're too hard on yourself. Our friends love you just as much as me. We're the perfect double act. Kara Edwards and Toby Saunders, together until the end of time."

My sister puts the serving plate on the table. The twins launch from their seats, almost knocking the orange juice over. You'd think they hadn't eaten in weeks. Anna, one of the twins, steals a crumpet or two most mornings before Helen starts cooking, and today is no different. The twins keep my sister on her toes, and I keep some of their secrets. They eat their breakfast, so there's no harm done.

Hayley spits her gum onto the table at the side of her plate. My nose wrinkles in distaste while Anna laughs. Toby is too busy studying the paper to notice.

"That's disgusting. Why are you chewing gum so early in the morning?" Helen asks.

The twins pull faces at each other while my sister continues to put the food on the table. My stomach growls with anticipation from the lingering aroma of fried bacon, sausage, and eggs. The second Helen's bottom touches the seat, we all grab for the food.

"The red sausages are the fire dragon batch from the butcher's. I warn you, they have a kick to them," Helen says.

Toby takes two of the new recipe sausages. I hesitate for a second before adding one to my plate. I cut off a small piece as I watch Toby take a big bite of his. He guzzles down some orange juice and takes another mouthful. The chilli warms my mouth on first contact. Feeling my face heat, I continue to take small chunks, chasing them down with gulps of cold milk.

"We can't take off for the whole summer. Who would help Helen with the twins?"

"We're old enough to look after ourselves. We start big school in September, remember?"

Rolling my eyes at Hayley's comment, I lean across the table for a slice of toast. Something wet and sticky hits my brown hair, stopping me mid-grasp. I don't have to be a genius to know Hayley threw her gum at me. My murderous gaze catches her fleeing body. My chair scrapes across the floor as I jump to my feet. Hayley is straight up the stairs and slamming her bedroom door shut before I even make it to the bannister. Redirecting, I head for the small downstairs bathroom to assess the damage.

Running my fingers through the knot in my hair, I locate the blue, sticky bubble gum. It squashes, entangling deeper into the strands of my hair. A groan leaves my lips as my sister appears in the doorway behind me with a jar of peanut butter in hand.

"I think scissors are my only option. Is the peanut butter to attract bees for my nest?"

"I'm sorry. The twins can be a handful, but Hayley will be sorry when I cut her pocket money. I've just looked online and it says peanut butter should entice the gum right out. It's worth a shot. Your curls are too beautiful to cut."

We're about the same height, so I duck my head down, giving my sister full access to the mess. A big dollop of nutty goo tickles my scalp. I cross my fingers for luck.

Please let this work.

"You're only eighteen once," Helen says, and I look at her curiously. "Don't have regrets because you've missed out on opportunities you should've taken. Go have fun with Toby. There's a summer sports club the girls said they wanted to try. It started a few days ago, but I'm going to give them a call and see if there's any space."

"I don't want to leave you."

"I have my girls. I won't be all by myself, and Derrick will be here at the weekends to help me out. Everything will be fine without you."

I like my sister's ex-boyfriend. Derrick is good with the twins and tries to see them as much as possible. I moved in with her around the time he left, so she could increase her hours at the sewing mill. I wanted to move out of my dad's place, so it worked out perfectly for us both. If I go with Toby, Helen will need someone to take care of my nieces during the week. My sister works long hours, and even though they're eleven, it's too long to be on their own.

Lancaster University is too far away for me to stay here longer than the summer, but I want to support my family as much as possible until I leave. Toby's adventure would be amazing. The only problem is, I won't leave my sister.

"I'm staying right here. There's nothing to discuss."

Helen teases my hair, and I watch in amazement as the gum slips straight out. She kisses my head before disappearing down the hall with the tub of peanut butter. Examining myself in the mirror, all traces of the gum have vanished, and I sigh with relief. My sister works her magic on another disastrous moment. She is like a modern-day witch, only her spell book is the internet.

I rinse the peanut butter out of my hair and dry it with a hand towel. Toby's brown eyes meet my blue ones through the reflection in the mirror. He runs his hand through his sandy blonde hair. When I turn to face him, he offers a weak smile, indicating that he already knows I'm going to reject his offer. A jolt of regret fills my stomach before I can get my words out.

"You know I need to stay close. We'll come up with a new plan even better than this one. Summer is going to be epic. All I want is you to be by my side and a few days of sunshine."

He towers over my small frame, placing his hands on my shoulders. He shakes me lightly before pulling me into a tight hug. "We'll work something out like we always do."

CHAPTER TWO

KARA

I freeze as the blue, water-filled balloon sails through the air, missing me by a small margin. The aftermath of the splash tickles my skin as it bursts on the wall behind me. My position is exposed, although I haven't spotted my attacker. I run for cover, keeping my head down. Crossing the grass, I take refuge behind the old playhouse. Catching a glimpse of familiar light brown curls, I creep up slowly behind Anna. She is peering out of the other side of the playhouse, unaware of my stealthy approach. My arm builds momentum, ready to launch the orange water bomb. A flicker of pink invades my vision before soaking my t-shirt with its contents. I close my eyes as the impact splatters up my neck.

Turning to face my attacker, I find a doe-eyed

Hayley, waiting for my reaction. She has her head down, but holds eye contact with me. Her arms are clasped together in a plea, and a frown plays across her glossy full lips.

"I'm sorry, Kara. I didn't think when I threw the gum. I'm such an idiot at times, but Mum says she got it all out. You've got to forgive me. I can't give up my favourite niece status."

She takes a step forward. I pull her into a hug, not caring that my t-shirt is probably wetting her pretty sundress. Even at eleven, she is almost as tall as me. It's one of the traits she gained from her father. The four of us all look similar to each other, with our blue eyes and curly brown hair. My sister and I are petite, whereas my nieces are leggier. I squeeze her a little harder.

"There's nothing to forgive. No damage is done. Let's forget the whole incident ever happened."

She's impulsive, but a good girl deep down. Her actions sometimes get her in trouble, although Anna tries to keep her in check.

"Hey! We both know I'm the favourite niece," Anna says. My back soaks with another direct hit of water. Laughing, I pull both girls into a bear hug, relishing the moment. The girls are too cool for affection most of the time these days. I have to take everything I can get. My smile deepens as they both hold on a little tighter.

"I thought we were having a water fight, not braiding each other's hair!" Toby shouts.

Looking around, I struggle to catch sight of him until a balloon splats inches away from my feet. Blocking out the sun with my hands, my gaze travels to the top of a nearby tree. I raise my eyebrow at the girls, pointing in Toby's direction.

"You're going down!" I shout.

We sprint for the pre-filled bucket and position it near the tree, taking turns to throw water bombs at Toby. He is high in the tree, and we don't manage to hit him with one single shot. He laughs every time we miss.

"I thought you were trying to wet me not give the tree a shower? You should water the tree roots if your aim is to help Mother Nature!"

"Don't worry, we'll get you," Hayley says.

By the time the bucket is empty, my sides hurt from all the laughter. The twins make a run for the outside tap as Toby hastily climbs down the tree. The second his feet touch the ground, he makes a beeline for the playhouse, but the girls are too quick for him. They pour the bucket over his head. He loses his footing, dramatically falling to the ground as the water splashes all over him.

"Pile on!" Hayley shouts between laughs.

Both girls leap on top of Toby, pinning him to the ground. Joining them is too tempting. I make my way over to them as Jordan, a boy we used to go to sixth form with, pulls open the creaky front gate. His blue Mohican stands out against the soft old country background. My eyes are drawn to his new skull tattoo which decorates his forearm. He rests a huge pile of leaflets against his chest, showing off his new ink. A smile spreads across my face as he waves at me with his free hand. Waving back, I change my direction, joining him on the garden path.

"What have you brought us?"

"The circus is coming to town, and these discount tickets have your name on them."

"How much are they paying you to deliver all those leaflets?"

"Not enough, although, according to my mum, it's an excuse to get me out of the house and off the game console for a few hours."

"At least you'll be able to use the money to buy a new game."

"You're definitely on to something there." He smiles widely.

Jordan hesitates as if he has something further to say. Instead, he hands me a leaflet before retreating back down the path. He keeps his eyes on me while slowly walking backwards. He points his index finger at me, tapping a tune out in the air. By the time I turn around, everyone is staring at me, waiting to see what I've got.

Holding up the bright yellow paper, I grin widely.

"We could go to the circus on Friday night. I know it's not a theme park, though it promises a night of entertainment. Anyone want to go?"

The circus comes to a nearby town once a year. My sister says it's a dying performance and buys tickets every time it visits. Usually, we all go together, but she will be working on Friday night. Still, I could take the girls with Toby.

Unenthusiastic grumbles from the group indicate they're less than impressed. Toby looks away, avoiding eye contact. A weak smile appears on my face while disappointment fills my stomach. It's not the reaction I'd hoped for.

I'm starting to feel cold from my damp clothes, so I collect my belongings from the wall and head inside. Taking a seat on the bed, I wrap my towel tightly around me. I hoped the circus would lighten the mood. I hate letting my best friend down. We do everything together, and usually I'm happy to follow his lead. His idea of heading off for the summer sounds great, but my sister is working extra hours to pay the bills. I can't just leave. Why does life get in the way? I would love to spend the summer at Blue Oaks. I could meet new people, and have the kind of adventure I've always wanted to have. But Helen doesn't need the stress of finding someone to watch over the girls. She needs me to be here. I'll have most of the day to myself once they join the summer club anyway. Hopefully, that will be enough for now. Toby is usually the one with the plan, but I have to come up with something, a silver-lining which will set everything back on track for summer.

A cold drip of water trickles from my hair and down my chest. I head to the bathroom and turn the shower on, and I step inside with two goals in mind. I need to clean up and think of a solid idea to pitch to Toby.

By the time I've put on my denim dungarees and a plain white t-shirt, I still haven't come up with anything. When I find the twins, they're in the kitchen, wrapped in their towels. Anna is dripping water on the floor while Hayley looks her unchanged perfect self.

"I call first dibs on the shower," Hayley says.

"You're hardly wet. You weren't even out there very long," Anna replies with a huff.

Hayley makes a run for the stairs at full speed. Anna lets out a frustrated groan while rubbing her hand over the back of her neck.

"I guess I'll wait. Thanks, Hayley," she mutters under her breath.

Offering a weak smile, I rub her back. We both know Hayley is the impatient twin. Anna is a saint in comparison. Looking around, I sense we're alone.

"Where's Toby?"

"He went home to change his clothes. He said he'd call you later."

Slumping down into the chair, I sigh with relief. At

least I have more time to come up with a plan. When I check my phone, there's an invite to a birthday party this weekend. It's another activity to add to our list, but I know it won't be enough to turn this summer around for Toby and me.

CHAPTER
THREE

BEAR

This is the only thing that means anything to me. Jumping from the edge of the half-pipe, I free-fall until the skateboard glides under my feet. My timing is perfect to give full momentum for my next trick.

As I move through the air, my smile grows. This is the only thing I've ever been good at. My heart settles with inner peace as I flip over into the eggplant trick, my hand grips the coping before I'm moving back down the half-pipe. It's easy to forget that I have an audience. At this moment, I'm free, even if it's only for a couple of minutes. Being on the road to teach groups of pre-teens is the happiest I've been all year. Skateboarding comes naturally to me. The boys and girls in front of me think I'm some kind of god. Their faces light up with an appreciation for my talent as I finish showing off.

"With a lot of practice, that will be you one day," I say as the skateboard comes to a stop. I flip it into my hand and head over to my group. "Let's start where we left off yesterday. We've got a few days to work up to the tricks. Split into groups of two and practice the jump balance technique I showed you."

Aaron, my teammate and close friend, pats me on the back as I remove my helmet. Pushing my brown hair out of my face, I turn to look at him, offering a head tilt. His own group is waiting for him on the dirt track.

"Your dad's on the phone," he says.

I roll my eyes while my lip screws up into an irritated snarl. It's not Aaron's fault, but I struggle to hide my frustration. Taking the phone from him, I bring it up to my ear. Sucking in a deep breath of air, I savour the moment before letting it go.

"Hey, Dad. I haven't got long to talk. How are you?"

"Julian, I've been trying to get hold of you for weeks. Where are you?" Nobody calls me Julian other than my dad. Bear is my circuit name and it helps me stay under the radar.

"We're in the north somewhere. Hull, maybe."

Aaron glances at the sign which states we're closer to Newcastle. Offering a shrug, I shake off my lie. The urban sports rota is on the internet. If my dad wanted to find me, he easily could. It wouldn't take five minutes to hunt me down, though I have no intention of spelling it out for him. I don't want to be found.

"I donate enough of my money to your projects. I think it's time you start investing in mine."

"I'm sorry, Dad. You're breaking up."

Running my finger over the speaker, I tap out a rhythm, trying to distort the sound. It's a cheap shot, and we both know it.

"Don't do this, Julian."

The line goes dead as my thumb rubs over the red circle which ends the call, and I toss the phone back to Aaron. There's a reason I left all electronic devices at home. I'm living on borrowed time with my dad. Now I'm eighteen, my responsibilities are catching up with me. This doesn't mean I'll return home without a fight. I wish he'd give me a break. My commitment to my future is something I can't avoid, although I'm trying really hard to postpone it.

"I'm sorry, Bear. I had no choice but to take the call. It could've been a potential sponsor and we need everything we can get."

"Don't worry about it. This is my problem."

Aaron is a great guy. He's five years older than me and wise beyond his years. He's dedicated his life to helping kids get into sports. We met when he first started setting up the underprivileged camp. The only good thing I've ever used my dad's money for is to help this project. The problem is, my dad gets his claws into me a little bit more each time. It's not enough that I'll be starting business studies at university in September. He has to ruin my whole summer too.

Running my hand through my hair, I excuse myself to use the bathroom. We're only in Northumberland for two weeks before we move onto the next youth centre. At least this one has a toilet block. The cold water washes over my skin, and I wipe my brow. Staring at my brown eyes in the mirror, I take a minute to get a hold of myself. If people knew my story, they would think I'm just some rich kid out to prove something. The truth is, I can't be the man my father wants me to be. I'm scared I might fail him, and failure is not an option.

Finding my baseball cap from the front seat of the van, I cover my messy hair. Back on the dirt track, Aaron is showing the kids his stunts. He's a professional cyclist who has won more awards than I can count. I've won a few skateboarding competitions, but my skills don't compare. When he catches sight of me, he finishes up his performance and strolls over to me.

After showing the group some simple techniques, the first few parents start to arrive. Soon, a slow stream of them gathers at the edge of the track.

"We'll pick this up in the morning. You're all dismissed. Have a good evening."

The group breaks into chatter as I pick up the equipment. Aaron joins me in the mad dash to get out of here. Living on the road isn't for everyone. To save costs, we're staying in a local hostel. There's no kitchen, so sandwiches and pasties have become our main diet. It's nothing like the east wing I'm accustomed to at home. My bathroom is bigger than the room we're sharing.

Dainty shoes appear in front of me as I collect the last knee pad. My gaze travels up her slender body until I return to a standing position. She's beautiful in a girl-next-door kind of way. Her pale skin and soft pink lips enhance her ocean blue eyes. When I catch her gaze, a flicker of confusion crosses her face. I hope she doesn't recognise me.

"Can I talk with you for a minute?" she asks. She must be related to one of the kids, but I'm not sure which one.

"How can I help?"

"My girls came today for a taster. They would like to sign up for the remainder of the sessions."

"I don't mean to be condescending, but you don't look old enough to have children in this class."

"They're my nieces, Hayley and Anna."

It takes me a couple of days to learn everyone's name. I vaguely remember two girls who look similar to the one standing before me.

"We start at nine in the morning. Try not to be late."

I check the ground for stray equipment, expecting the cute brunette in front of me to be done, but when she makes no attempt to move, I raise an eyebrow at her. She rubs her thumb across her forearm, fidgeting like she has something on her mind.

"I'll try to be on time."

I don't think that's what she wanted to say, but she doesn't give me a chance to question her. She turns and runs across the track into the car park. After she disappears out of sight, I take the equipment to the van.

"What was that all about?" Aaron asks.

"I'm not sure. All I know is she will be back tomorrow."

He shrugs indifferently to the news. Helping these kids and their families is what this programme is all about. We might only be a two-week break from their parents having to keep them entertained, but I aim to inspire.

Aaron starts the engine, and it isn't long until we're back at the hostel. The room we share is basic and lacks any kind of luxury. Every single footstep echoes against the cold, hard floor. The bed creaks as Aaron takes a seat on the edge. He seems lost in thought as he stares out of the small, dirty window.

"Do you want to talk about it?" I ask.

"Shouldn't I be the one asking you that question?"

"My dad calling doesn't change a thing. You knew my situation when I joined you."

This summer was supposed to be about me taking back some control. I love my dad, but he's suffocating me. It's not like I can truly escape my legacy, but would one last adventure hurt?

"I've been calculating the cost of the summer. The numbers are short even without me giving you a wage."

"Don't even consider it. I would never take your money."

"You've done more than enough for me and the charity. I need to come up with a new way to entice sponsors. I'm going to take some flyers to the circus on Friday if you want to join me."

"I'll help you give out leaflets. It's a start. We'll come up with something to give the donation pot a boost. How much are you short?"

He runs his hands through his dirty blonde hair. A look of pain washes over his face.

"It's enough to consider sleeping in the van."

CHAPTER

FOUR

KARA

Friday arrives too quickly, and I haven't managed to come up with any good ideas. I'm not used to being the instigator. Toby is usually the one with the ideas. He hasn't liked any of my suggestions so far, and I've seen him eyeing up the theme park advertisements. If only Halloween took place in summer, then we'd have Scare-fest, which is kind of like a haunted house.

"Kara, I'm heading out," my sister shouts from downstairs, breaking me from my daydream. I chase after her as she opens the front door.

"We're setting off to the circus in half an hour."

"Yes, Anna told me. Do you need some money?"

"I have some left from the supermarket."

"If you call me, I'll pick you up after the performance. Have fun." She kisses my cheek and curses when she sees the time on her watch. Like a whirlwind, she rushes out the door. Toby appears in her place moments later.

"I know I'm early. Can I borrow your laptop? Mine's a goner."

"Sure, help yourself."

He strides up the stairs two at a time. I follow slowly. The girls are out of the bathroom, and the aroma of sweet strawberry almost chokes me. I knock once on their bedroom door before I enter.

"Are you girls almost ready?"

"I can't find my blue jumper," Hayley says while pulling her clothes out of the drawers.

Sliding the wardrobe door, I find the sweater neatly folded on a shelf inside. I give it to her as I comb through my hair using the mirror on the door. Anna is already dressed and reading a book on her bed.

By the time we arrive at the circus, we only have a few minutes to spare. The big top is already filling up. We take our seats while Toby tries to flag down the snack vendor. The scent of burnt popcorn and engine oil brings back sweet childhood memories of excitement.

The girls wave at a group of their friends. Disappearing into the crowd, they go to join them, leaving me sitting with Toby. Taking a handful of popcorn, I sit on the bench, waiting for the show to start.

My attention drifts to a guy in a black hoody and baseball cap, it's Bear. I've heard the name before, but only as a modern day baby name. He looks about my age which is too old for a name like that. He stops to talk to the girls and their friends. Toby brings me out of my daydream by nudging my foot.

"Maybe I should join the circus. At least it'd get me out of this town and on my way to an adventure," he says.

"Are you that desperate to get out of here?"

"I want more. The end of sixth form was supposed to be the start of something better. Nobody mentioned having to wait around."

A flash of blue hair appears in my eye-line as Jordan sits next to me. He saves me from being a broken record by apologising to Toby for the millionth time. I don't want to hold him back, but I can't just up and leave my family.

"I knew you two wouldn't let me down. Those tickets really did have your name on them."

He unfastens the top button of his checked shirt, rocking back in his seat. It isn't warm in here. If anything, there's a draught. He keeps his attention on the arena, even though it's empty.

"I've been meaning to ask you if you've made plans for tomorrow night. There's a new spy film I'd like to see if you're interested in going?" Jordan asks with a nervous edge to his voice.

"It's Rebecca's birthday party. We're planning on going, right, Toby? Maybe we can catch the movie another time."

"Sure. Sounds great."

The dazzling lights dart around the arena, signalling the show is about to begin. Toby leans in to whisper in my ear.

"You know he just asked you on a date?"

Jerking my body back so I can study his face, I shake my head. He nods at me with a smug expression. Jordan has never shown any interest in me in that way. I try to forget Toby's comment as the ringmaster draws my attention back to the stage.

Each performance is more daring than the last. Every flip, spin, and somersault wows the crowd. This never gets old for me. I love every minute, though I can't help feeling a little sad. I'm going to miss everything about this town when we leave at the end of the summer.

The new black hatchback that picks us up isn't the car we're expecting. Derrick is in the driver's seat, and there's no sign of my sister. The girls run to greet their father. I wave goodbye to the guys and make my way to the car.

"Where's Helen?"

"She's running late. You know how it can be with her sometimes. It's good to see you all. My week has been too long and boring. I've missed my babies."

"Dad, we're all grown up now," Hayley says.

"That you are, slugger. Now, let's go get ice cream on the way home."

The girls cheer as we set off. My eyes narrow at

Derrick, but he doesn't turn to look at me; he stays focused on the road. He's a clockwork kind of guy. It's unusual for him to break his pattern. My sister never mentioned him coming and I'm suspicious.

Helen is eating a sandwich in the kitchen when we arrive home. The girls settle in front of the television with their ice creams. Making myself a cup of tea, I try to subtly catch my sister's attention. The front door clicks, letting me know Derrick has entered the house.

"Tea, anyone?" I say.

"No, thank you," Helen replies.

Nobody speaks while I wait for the kettle to boil. I take a cup out of the cupboard, trying my best to be quick. Derrick has his arms crossed and my sister keeps her head down. Filling my cup with hot water, I give the tea a second to brew. Time ticks too slowly, and Derrick begins to pace. I've outstayed my welcome by the time milk enters my cup. I grab my tea and get the hell out of there. My room is actually Derrick's old study, but it's the only space I have.

Settling the cup on the desk, I lift the lid on my laptop. My eyebrows knit together as confusion fills my mind. The screen shows the Blue Oaks website. I haven't looked at this. The cogs in my brain begin to turn until the pieces click into place. Toby.

Voices downstairs draw my attention away from the screen. Creeping to the top of the stairs, I cup my ear to listen to the conversation.

"I want to be closer to my girls. It'll only be a couple of weeks while I get back on my feet. Please, Helen."

"Can't you stay with one of your friends?"

"It makes sense for me to be here. Everything I want is in this house."

"Where are you going to sleep?"

"The couch. Anywhere. It doesn't matter."

"You've got two days."

"Give me until the end of next week."

"Fine."

My sister appears in the hall. She spots me, instantly stopping in her tracks. She raises her hands in the air, shaking her fists with frustration.

"What am I supposed to do?"

I hold my hands up in defence. "Hey, I'm not judging."

She rubs her arm over her forehead. "Would you mind sharing a room with me, so Derrick can stay in the study? It'll be like when we were kids."

Averting my eyes, I hesitate before suggesting a solution I don't want to consider. "I could stay with Dad."

"Don't you dare! Moving out of Dad's place was the right decision. Living with him isn't an option, not to mention his girlfriend will drive you insane. We'll manage. It's only for a few days."

"I'll go grab my stuff."

Helen disappears into the living room with a dark

aura following her. Filling my bags with clothes and essentials, I drag it across the hall. Living with Allison, my dad's girlfriend, isn't a realistic option. The woman is worse than a hangover headache. My relationship with my dad has always been sketchy, and living with him was difficult. It would be a last resort to move in with them. Settling into my sister's bed, I find a movie to stream.

I hear the girls let out an excited squeal. I'm guessing they're happy their dad will be staying with us. I just hope they don't get their hopes up. I hated seeing them disappointed when he left.

CHAPTER FIVE

KARA

The party is in full swing when we arrive. Music blasts out of the sound system playing the latest Ed Sheeran song and people are spread across the grass in small groups. A cloud of whirling smoke fills the air around the barbecue. Rebecca stands on the garden table. Her hands are on her hips as she talks to the crowd around her.

Toby pulls me through the sea of drunken bodies, making our way to the kitchen. He locates a bottle opener, popping the lid off the apple cider. Using a large serving ladle, I help myself to a paper cup of punch. It's an unhealthy green, although it doesn't taste too bad.

A couple of guys from school high-five Toby as they pass through.

Toby and I play ping pong in the cellar. Most of

the party stays outside. Toby is good friends with Kyle, Rebecca's brother, so he knows the hideouts. I hit the ball over the net with ease and Toby bats it back. I begin to feel a sense of déjà vu.

"Do you ever feel like we're in a holding ground, waiting for the next chapter to begin?" I ask.

"That's what I've been trying to tell you. It's the same thing just a different day. If I walk upstairs right now, I could join a game of spin the bottle or poker. I could kiss my ex-girlfriend, and then spend the next week avoiding her calls. The night would be fun, don't get me wrong. All of it, except avoiding my ex, of course. I've already got that t-shirt. This summer is supposed to be a final farewell, yet since sixth form ended, I feel like I'm waiting on the edge. Ready for the next step, but unable to take it."

"I know what you mean. It's just complicated for me," I say, my voice trailing off at the end.

"I understand, I really do. But the theme park is less than an hour away from Lancaster University. It's a step closer to the future. A step I can't wait to take. It could open up possibilities for extra cash in the holidays, and maybe weekends too."

"I want to go, I really do, but..."

He holds up his hands, letting the ping pong ball fly off the table, and I cheer.

"So that's how it's going to be. Distracting me for cheap shots. You better bring it because it's on."

He hits the ball hard across the ping pong table,

and I knock it back with equal force. Lunging forward, I hit the ball, barely getting it over the net. Toby hits it back with ease. The ball spins through the air, heading straight off the corner of the table.

"Yes!" Toby laughs while fist-pumping the air.

"Mind if I cut in?" Kyle asks.

Kyle and Jordan must've made their way into the basement while I was engrossed in the game. Throwing the paddle down on the table, I move away.

"Take my place. He's cheating anyway."

Toby lets out a fake laugh. "Sore loser."

A smile creeps onto my face.

Resting my back against the wall, I settle in next to Jordan. He's as tall as Toby, making me feel small.

"How was the movie?" I say.

"I didn't go. I'm hoping you're free tomorrow?" Jordan asks.

The amber light flicks on in my head when I meet Toby's gaze. "We could all go. I'm sure Toby will be up for it."

Jordan places his arm gently on mine, grabbing my attention. "I'm thinking just me and you could go?"

"Like a date?"

He nods.

Toby already warned me this is what Jordan was trying to say yesterday and I didn't listen. I've never had a serious boyfriend. The few dates I've been on have never turned into anything more. Call me old-fashioned, but I want something I haven't felt yet.

The butterflies they talk about in books. I want a spark of something magical that ignites a fire inside. Jordan has never even given me a tingle.

"Why now?"

"You're always with Toby. I thought maybe there was something going on. Now I'm running out of time, so I wanted to at least try because I've always had a crush on you."

"Toby and I are just friends. Nothing more."

"It's hard for a guy to try and impress you when you're always with him."

I do spend all my free time with Toby. We've always been close, like brother and sister. If I was interested, I'd have made time to get to know Jordan. I don't want to hurt his feelings, but being honest with him is all I can offer.

"I'm with Toby a lot because he's my best friend. I'm sorry, but you and I can't lead anywhere. We're both moving to opposite sides of England in a few months."

His shoulders slump slightly, and he bends his head forward avoiding looking at me. Running my hand through my hair, I struggle with my words. The room begins to feel hot and I need to get out of here for some fresh air.

"I'm sorry," I say, trying to sound sincere. I don't want any bad feelings between us. I like Jordan, just not in that way.

The walls feel as though they're closing in around

me. The building seems smaller than it did five minutes ago. I struggle through the sea of warm bodies making my way out of the house. When the cold breeze hits my face, I can breathe more easily. Laughter and chatter echo around the garden which makes me smile sadly. These people have been my friends for years. This town is all I've ever known. Just like Toby, I'm ready to start the next chapter, although taking the actual step is scary. Having the people I love close to me is a comfort. I don't let many people get close. Jordan's words are true; I do choose to stay with Toby. He's my safety net. It doesn't mean I don't want to meet a guy; it just has to be the right one.

Glancing back at the party, I see Bear in his black hoodie, holding his skateboard. He's talking to a couple of local guys. It's like he senses me. His gaze locks with mine, but he doesn't say hello. We stare at each other for way too long before I break eye contact. Goose pimples have appeared on my skin and I pull my cardigan down over my forearms. When I look back up, Bear is no longer in sight. I send an apologetic text to Toby for bailing on him and take a slow walk home.

These streets are as familiar to me as the back of my hand. This is where I grew up. Some of my best childhood memories happened here, and until recently, I never thought I'd leave. When Toby suggested we go to university, I was unsure at first.

Now, when I look around, I'm noticing how predictable my life would be if I stayed here. It isn't a bad thing, but I wonder if there could be more for me.

A new sense of dread comes over me when I reach my house. Something isn't right. The lights are shining bright, the curtains are open, and there's movement in the downstairs windows. It's after the girls' bedtime and my stomach fills with dread. The front door slams a little too loudly behind me, and Hayley runs down the stairs, pulling me into a tight hug.

"You're home."

I frown in confusion. "Why aren't you asleep?"

She points to the living room as an explanation. The door is closed, and I don't want to enter what can only be a bad situation. My gaze finds Anna at the top of the stairs. She has her arms wrapped around the spindles and her head is poking out.

Tucking Hayley under my arm, I lead her upstairs. We push the girls' beds together. Grabbing my laptop, I find a romantic comedy movie, and we snuggle up to watch it. This is our ritual when Helen works late, or something is bothering them.

"Anyone want to tell me what's going on?"

"Dad says he wants to move back in," Hayley says.

"Oh. What did your mum say?"

"I don't think I should repeat it. Something about a dead body."

"It will work itself out. I promise." I offer her a weak smile while comforting her with a hug.

The girls drift off to sleep before the end of the movie, but I'm wide awake. The house is silent. Whatever happened before I got home has already ended. The unresolved argument hangs thick in the air, though. Any chance of leaving before the end of summer is gone. I'm needed here to support my family.

It may have been Toby who suggested us going to university, but my sister encouraged me to apply. I'll be the first member of our family to attend and I want it badly, but it's overwhelming to think I'll be leaving all this behind. When the acceptance letter came, I couldn't believe I'd got a place. Ever since my mum left, Helen and I have always looked out for each other. Now I feel selfish for wanting to follow my dreams when there's so much more I could do here.

The hallway plunges into darkness, and my sister's door clicks into place. I listen to the sounds of her footsteps as she potters around her room. My eyes feel heavy while I try to fight my inevitable sleep, and it isn't long until I drift off.

CHAPTER SIX

BEAR

"That's a wrap for today, guys. You did a great job."

The second Monday of any two week block is always my favourite. The kids who have truly enjoyed learning the sport have practiced all weekend and their confidence is beginning to shine through.

Picking up the green crate, I begin to collect the equipment. The group fizzles out until there are only a few stragglers left. The mystery girl I seem to be seeing everywhere stands at the edge of the field. Her nieces run to her, hugging her tightly. She whispers something to them before her eyes find me. I'm staring. I can't help myself. My feet take on a life of their own and I soon find my way across to them.

"I hope you girls are enjoying the skateboard lessons," I say.

"I didn't fall off once today," Anna says with pride.

"I'll make a skater out of you yet."

"Do you offer adult lessons? Kara needs a new hobby," Hayley says.

Kara's a pretty name for a beautiful girl. It suits her. When I look at her face, she's glaring at Hayley. I get the feeling Kara isn't interested in learning my tricks.

"Unfortunately, I'm only here until the end of the week. You could show your aunt some of your moves."

"We aren't very good yet," Anna says.

"If you want to impress somebody, maybe you need more lessons too."

"I can't believe you said that, Hayley."

The girls run off into the car park, chasing each other, giggling.

"The twins have their own language sometimes. Ignoring their cryptic messages is the only way to stay sane," Kara says.

"I know skateboarding or cycling probably isn't their first choice of activity, but they're both doing well."

She brushes a strand of hair away from her face while she seems to consider my words. "This has been good for them. How did you get into this job?"

"I've been skating since I was little and it came easy to me. When I was in my early teens, I started competing in extreme sport competitions. That's where I met Aaron. He was dominating the score-board with his mad skills and had big dreams for the prize money. His energy was inspiring and I wanted to help him out."

"It must be nice to have a purpose."

I look out into the distance. When my attention focuses back on Kara I try to put on an easy-going smile. "Being a free spirit without any responsibility would be awesome."

"When you're skating, you look free to me."

My eyes search hers. What does this girl see when she looks at me? Could it be more than others see? I shake off the thought. If I had the choice, I would skate for hours. Kara can probably see my enthusiasm for skating, nothing more.

"You should give it a try. It could be the new hobby the girls suggested you need. If you're serious about the lesson, I could work something out."

If I can offer an escape for anyone, even for a couple of hours, I'm happy to help.

"I'll talk to my partner in crime, Toby, and see if I can get a few people on board."

Of course she has a boyfriend. It shouldn't matter to me, yet I feel disappointed. On the other hand, since when has anyone referred to their boyfriend as a partner-in-crime?

Pulling a leaflet from my back pocket, I hand it to her. Our fingers touch briefly and I try to block out the tingle I get from touching her soft skin.

"Aaron is the main guy, so if you change your mind,

contact him. We're here until Sunday and happy to earn some extra cash for the charity."

———

Taking my time, I stroll through the park, handing out a few leaflets. I untuck my jumper from around my waist and pull it over my head; the temperature is dropping as a cold breeze sets in. The wind lightly blows the leaves and the bright light from the sun catches my face between the trees. The park is an easy place to find supporters as the half-pipe draws in the right crowd. I manage to strike up conversations with a few dog walkers who reminisce about their younger skater days. I stay for a couple of hours, and when I reach the hostel, the sun is already starting to set. Aaron's grey transit van is parked up, and the light is on in our room. Knocking on the door, I wait for him to answer.

The sound of Aaron's footsteps echo as he approaches the door. He pushes it open, not looking up from his phone. He excuses himself to use the bathroom without a second glance. I lay on the bed with my hands under my head, watching the shadows from the street lights move across the room. The sound of the running water from the shower relaxes me. My eyes are heavy, and I close them just for a moment. The swing of the bathroom door startles me as Aaron appears back in the room, dressed in his lounge pants.

"Have we had any response from the leaflet drops?" I say, rubbing my tired eyes.

Between the two of us, we've covered a couple of miles. I started with a few business estates, but I also covered some houses and parks too.

"Nothing has come of it yet."

"I've distributed a hundred plus leaflets tonight. I found a large industrial estate."

He swallows, combing his hands through his hair. After pacing around the space, he sits on the end of my bed. "There's no easy way to tell you this, so I'm just going to say it. Your dad's in town, and he's playing dirty."

I suck in a deep breath before I respond. My father never plays fair, so I wouldn't expect anything less. He likes to get his own way. We only have each other, so I don't want this to be a wedge between us, but I don't want to be controlled.

"What did he offer you?"

"Nothing's worth our friendship. I told him to shove his money and I can't be bought."

Aaron's always been loyal, and it's nice to know he appreciates me.

"Good. At least I have something to bargain with."

We both know Aaron can't dismiss his donation, even on principle. My father always says everyone has a price, and it's just about finding the right number.

CHAPTER SEVEN

KARA

This recipe book is probably older than me. The corners are covered thick with baking mixture. If my grandmother didn't swear by these instructions, I'd suggest buying Helen a new cookbook. Hayley appears from the pantry with the flour while Anna grabs the eggs and milk from the fridge. The pink icing and candy decorations are on the top shelf of the cupboard. The basket of cake lettering falls as I pull them out and they scatter on the floor while I climb back down from the work surface.

"These are going to be the best fairy buns ever made. I just found some pink butterfly cases," Hayley says, waving them in the air.

"I have the sprinkles," I reply.

"And I've got the retro eighties music," Anna adds.

I hold up my arm and we slap a round of high-fives to celebrate. A cloud of dust follows our cheers.

"How did you manage to get flour on your hands before we've even started baking?" I ask Hayley.

"Sorry. That's the secret ingredients. It's edible pink glitter, not flour. It fell out of the cupboard when you were trying to break the baking supplies."

"I wasn't trying to break anything."

My foot slips on a bottle I've missed on the floor. The girls laugh as I perform my own circus balancing trick.

Together, we work the ingredients into the bowl. Glitter and food colouring surrounds the baking mix like a love potion.

Anna laughs. "Kara, you've got fairy gloop on your face."

Grabbing the towel, I try to remove it. The giggles tell me I've made it worse.

"Here, let me help," Hayley says. The cold mixture slides down my face.

"You did not just do that!"

Chasing her with a sprinkle of flour, I throw it in her direction, covering some of her hair. Laughing, we chase each other around the kitchen. There's more flour on the floor than in the bowl. Glitter is sparkling from every surface; it looks like a five-year-old's birthday party exploded everywhere.

"These buns aren't going to cook themselves," Anna says.

Saluting her, I place the baking tray into the oven and set the timer.

"Anna's just grumpy because the boy she likes hasn't texted her today."

"What boy?" I can't hide the surprise in my voice. They are growing up too fast. It was only a few weeks ago I was dropping them off at junior school.

"There's no boy!" Anna screeches.

"Jasper," Hayley tells me.

"Who's Jasper?" I ask.

Anna's eyes widen. "Nobody."

"He's from the summer club." The corners of Hayley's lips twitch, revealing a mischievous smile.

Anna's cheeks glow red. "I'm actually going to kill you."

The girls go for another round of flour wars. White powder flutters around the room and laughter escapes from my lips with ease. Dipping my finger into the bowl, I taste the raw mixture. I love moments like this when nobody's watching and we can just mess around. Once the girls start school, they'll grow up and won't want to do things like this with me anymore.

Leaving them to their play fight, I make my way into the living room and collapse onto the sofa. My sides hurt from laughing too hard. The girls join me, leaving a trail of flour in their wake. I pull them in close to me, watching the mess spread over the cushions. A little flour never hurt anyone; I'll clear it up later.

"Come on, spill the gossip. I'm dying to know all about Jasper," I say, rubbing my hands together.

"We'll be going to school together in September. It's not a big deal," Anna says in a quiet voice. Her hands fidget in her lap.

"He keeps looking at Anna whenever he thinks we're not watching," Hayley says.

"I don't blame him. He would be lucky to be friends with one of my beautiful girls."

"He's okay for a nerd." Hayley pulls up a picture from the summer club on her phone. A fresh-faced pre-teen comes into view. He looks like Anna's type of friend.

"He's cute."

Anna covers her face with a pillow while Hayley raises her eyebrow at me. The girls really are growing up. Cutting Anna some slack, I change the subject. If she wants to tell me about the mystery boy, she will in time.

"Shall we watch a movie?"

"I'm voting for *A Cinderella Story*. *Lizzie McGuire* may be old news, but I love Hilary Duff," Anna says.

"What about you, Kara? When are you going to bring a boy home?" Hayley asks.

"Toby was here yesterday."

"You know what I mean."

"I'm waiting for my prince. I want the whole nine

yards. A magical foot-popping kiss has to happen before I would bring anyone home to meet my girls."

"Do you think the foot-popping kiss actually happens outside the movies?" Anna asks.

"Absolutely. There's no rush for first kisses. Finding the right person is more important."

"How romantic. I want that too," Hayley says.

———

The red-checked cloth flows over the freshly cleaned table. After lighting the pastel love heart candles, I place them at the centre of the table. Stirring the stew one more time, I turn the gas off. My stomach rumbles while my mouth waters at the aroma of cooked vegetables. Helen should be home any minute.

It took over an hour to get rid of every last trace of glitter, and I'm pretty certain it didn't wash out of my hair. The kitchen is sparkling for a whole different reason now, though.

The front door opens and the girls barrel down the stairs.

"Mum's home," they shout in unison.

"What's got into you two?" Helen asks.

With the spoon still in my hand, I peer around the kitchen door to find my family in a group hug. Helen looks surprised.

"I hope you're hungry. We've made a special tea," I say.

"How did I get so lucky?"

The smile on my face is instant as my sister licks her lips. The hours of cooking and cleaning were worth the happy look. Waving the spoon, I invite them into the kitchen.

"Food's ready."

I fill bowls with the homemade stew, placing them on the table.

"I've got a surprise for you too," Helen says.

"Me?"

"It won't be long until you start university and I wanted to make you a thank you present."

She places the brown wrapped parcel on the table. Raising my eyebrow, I eye the gift. Who am I kidding? I can't wait any longer. Ripping the paper from the present, I unveil an oilcloth pencil case with my sister's logo on the edge. She wants to start her own brand of custom made items, except she's never found enough time.

"I love it! It's going to look so good on my desk. Thank you." I put the pencil case on the table. It'll be nice to have a little piece of my sister with me. My stomach growls. "Let's eat already. I'm starving."

I don't wait for anyone to answer as I spoon a large amount of vegetables into my mouth.

"Where's Dad?" Anna asks.

"He's looking for a place to rent nearby, so he can see you girls more often."

My eyes meet Helen's across the table, however, I

don't comment. A phone chimes, indicating someone has a text message.

"No phones at the table," Helen says.

Hayley scoops up the phone while Anna launches towards her. Casually, I walk around the table and grab the phone from Hayley. Both girls freeze. Helen looks between us in confusion. Glancing at the screen, my suspicion is confirmed.

"The girls are enjoying the summer club, that's all. I'm taking them back tomorrow before I meet Toby."

I try to act causal, but the moment I stop talking, all eyes turn to Helen.

"What have I missed?" Helen narrows her eyes.

"Nothing," Anna and I say too hastily.

"Anna has a boyfriend." Hayley smiles angelically.

"I do not. Take that back." Anna huffs while Hayley shrugs.

"Anna has a crush."

"My girls are too young to have crushes." The shock in Helen's voice is undeniable.

"It's going to happen, Mum. Besides, there are some cute boys at the summer club. I think even Kara has a crush on the instructor."

I can't hide the shock on my face. Bear's easy on the eye, I can admit to myself, but I didn't think my attraction was obvious. It doesn't mean I have any interest in him. Besides, he will be gone at the end of the week.

After a round of extra sparkly buns, the girls go to

choose their outfits for tomorrow. Both are more than excited about meeting their new friends. Our busy day has made them sleepy and they're ready to go to bed.

I settle on the sofa next to Helen.

"Thank you," she says with a lazy smile. "I needed tonight."

"Would it be so bad if Derrick moved back in on a temporary basis?" I asked.

"I can't do it. We're doing so well on our own. I know I'm leaning on you for support, but we've made it this far. Going backwards isn't an option. He can't just turn up and expect everything to fall into place for him."

"Maybe I should defer for a year."

"Don't you dare! You need to live your own life."

We give each other a hug. What my sister is saying is true, even though it's hard to let go. I want to be there for her, but she's right. I shouldn't put my future on hold.

CHAPTER EIGHT

KARA

Climbing the spiral staircase two steps at a time, I race to the top. The familiar vibrations echo under my feet. The smell of freshly laundered clothes brings back fond memories of playing in this house. I pass the beautiful artwork I've seen a hundred times before. My gaze only lingers for a few moments on each piece, until I reach my favourite picture. It's an oil painting of Toby and me when we were seven. His mum is a talented artist. A smile spreads across my face at the memory of that winter's day. I enter Toby's room to find him relaxing on his bed with his big feet hanging over the edge.

"Move up. Make some room for a little one," I say.

"Did you see my mum in the kitchen?"

I launch myself onto the soft duvet. Toby is an

only child. He has a huge bed which matches his enormous room.

"Yes. She's bringing milk and cookies up."

He rolls his eyes. Toby is close with his mum, even if he doesn't like to admit it, and Penny is a sweetie. Right on cue, she enters the room with a tray of snacks. She offers me a biscuit before placing the rest on the desk. Her smile is bright and full of cheer, though her eyes are silently communicating with Toby. She doesn't speak as she leaves the room.

"You should be nice to your mum. She makes the best treats."

As I take a bite of my biscuit, Toby frowns. "How come she offers you the tray and I've got to get my own food?"

"They're right there on the desk."

As he gets up, I quickly steal his warm spot on the duvet. I'm predictable. We both knew I would do it, just like every other time. Toby turns on the television, searching through the channels. He returns to the bed, trying to push me out of his seat.

"I won't be able to see the television with your big butt in the way."

He rolls his eyes and retreats for the tray, placing it on the bottom of the bed. Instead of sitting next to me, he perches on the edge of the mattress. Narrowing my eyes, I watch him suspiciously as he taps his fingers against his thigh and pretends to be engrossed in the movie we've seen millions of times before. Usually Toby wouldn't be so quiet while we watch a film.

"What's up with you?"

"Why did you turn Jordan down? You said you'd like a summer romance. He's a nice guy. Why didn't you want him to take you out for a date or two?"

"Is this where you confess your undying love for me?" My lips curl up in a smirk.

"Wouldn't life be so much easier if I did?" He raises an eyebrow.

A few seconds pass before we both burst out laughing. It would be *so* much easier if Toby and I had feelings for each other. I wouldn't have to deal with his crazy ex-girlfriends, which has happened too many times to count. I'm like his own personal bodyguard when situations have got out of hand. He's good at picking the intense ones, which was taken to the extreme with his last relationship. Emma used to call me every day to find out why he hadn't returned her calls. Maybe that's why we never dated; I'm too laid back. Since the day we met, Toby and I have been best friends. We bonded over our daddy issues, and we've stuck together ever since. As friends, we've been to a school dance or two together. I make a fabulous fake girlfriend to get him out of a tight spot, but there has never been anything more. There's no spark. No secret feelings towards each other. It's simple; we work perfectly the way we are.

"Being my best friend has its perks too. I always have your back."

"You're the closest thing to a sister I've ever had. I want you to be happy. I like having you to myself, but I know, eventually, you'll find someone."

"As much as I'd like to tell you all about my non-existing dating life, I'll be your faithful sidekick for a little longer."

"One date with Jordan might be what you need."

I screw my face up. "Why are you pushing this?"

He runs his fingers through his hair. "I applied for the theme park job."

Sitting up a little straighter, I give Toby my full attention. He has never been a straight talker. If he's telling me about a job, it's probably because he's already got it. "When do you leave?"

He runs his hand over his mouth. "In a couple of days."

"Congratulations. I'm really happy for you."

My smile falls into place, although we both know I'm a little sad. This will be the longest we've ever been apart. I usually follow Toby everywhere.

"It's only a couple of weeks and then we'll be back together."

"I know. I'm being silly." I wipe the single tear which warms my cheek as he pulls me into a hug. "This is so girly of me. I'm sorry. I know it's only a few weeks and holding you back isn't what I want."

"The offer is still there. Come with me."

"You know I can't."

Toby wants this. I won't stand in his way. The signs were all there right from the start. It was selfish of me to think he would want to stay here for me.

"Maybe you should give Jordan a shot. It can't hurt, right?"

"When I'm interested in a guy, I won't be playing hard to get. Jordan isn't my type. You can't pawn me off that easily. You owe me."

"Yeah, I know. Unicorns don't grow on trees, but I'll try my best."

His promise of a unicorn runs back to Year Six. The first time he wanted something from me. He should've offered his mum's cookies up for bait. Someday, I'm going to cash in on that unicorn.

"Let's enjoy the time we have. No more of this sad talk."

I rub my hands over my face before helping myself to another biscuit. The tray contains enough sugary snacks to feed an army of girl scouts.

"How much time do we have until you need to pick up the twins?"

"We have a couple of hours."

"Let's go to our special place."

I slip a few extra treats into my pocket before following Toby out of the door.

———

Walking along the wooden log, I make my way into the forest with Toby hot on my tail. We've had some of our best memories in these woods.

"What's so special about Blue Oaks?" I ask. When he doesn't answer straight away, I turn to face him.

"I've been talking to someone." He rubs his shoulder awkwardly, like he doesn't want to admit this.

"Let me get this right, you're leaving me for a girl?" I give him a stern look.

"Not just a girl. After we saw the advert in the paper, I started looking into the jobs and came across Sophie on Instagram. She's taken some interesting pictures around the park and I wanted to know more so I started messaging her."

I give him a knowing look. How good can her pictures of the scenery be to make him so interested? I bet she's pretty, which makes me want to roll my eyes. He's so easily distracted by a cute girl.

"Let me guess, she's looking for a summer fling."

"It's not like that. I've never felt this way before." He runs his hands through his hair, like he does when he's trying to be serious.

"Could the commitment-phobic Toby Saunders be hung up on a girl?"

He laughs, averting his eyes. "I'm not that bad. It isn't my fault my past relationships haven't worked out. Sophie is different; she wants to go backpacking around Europe. She has zero interest in settling down anytime soon and we're like-minded. Sophie is all about having adventures, just like me."

Sounds like he's been talking to her a lot.

"Let's hope you can cope without your best friend."

"I can handle it. If it gets crazy, I'll be back here before you know it."

I laugh. It's typical of Toby to run away from conflict. Girls are good at scaring him off.

The big sycamore tree comes into view and I run towards it at full speed. Toby is just as quick to follow in my footsteps. Whenever I want to escape home, this is the place Toby can find me. It's our secret hideout.

The wooden notches are worn into flat steps from years of climbing the tree. Taking a steady path, I climb to the top. The only sounds are from the birds and swaying tree branches. Pulling myself up onto the manmade lookout point, I take my familiar seat. Toby isn't far behind me. We look out into the forest, listening to its call. The smell of damp wood and mud makes me feel peaceful.

"You're not angry with me, are you?"

My head swings round to look at Toby. "Don't be daft. Of course I'm not. I'll miss you, but I want you to go."

"Oh, so you want to get rid of me?"

I knock him off balance. This is why we work so well together. We know how far we can push each other. At first, I was upset Toby was leaving, but it's for the best. He wants a summer I can't offer him, and I won't hold him back.

CHAPTER NINE

BEAR

My skateboard turns 360 degrees in the air as my feet move into position for the kickflip landing. This is the last trick of the day. These kids are looking at me like I just grew two heads. I slow down my movement, building momentum but not actually taking my feet off the board. Jasper's the first one to successfully flip the skateboard and land back on his feet. It's great to see my teaching methods rubbing off on the kids.

"Beginner's luck," Hayley shouts.

Jasper's second attempt ends with him sitting on the floor as laughter echoes around the group. I reach out to help him up. His ears turn bright red as he takes my hand, pulling himself up.

Once the group settles down, I start to explain the next trick. A sound in the background makes me pause, and it's nothing to do with the children.

My breath hitches for a second as I run my hand down my arm. The group's attention is drawn away from me, even as I perform another effortless kick-flip, ignoring the increasing noise.

My dad has called Aaron more times than I can count. I offered to buy him a new phone, even though it was an unrealistic solution. He needs his number to be easy to find.

The propellers begin to slow as the engine cuts out. All the kids are lost in the mystery of our guest. I mutter a curse under my breath, only loud enough for me to hear.

The pilot emerges from the far side of the helicopter to open the passenger door. My old man gracefully climbs out with his cane in hand. His brown eyes latch on to me immediately. After smartening his suit, he limps carefully over the grass towards me.

I can't put this off any longer. The children stare with their mouths open as my dad approaches. I can't muster any kind of welcome. My eyes never leave his face. My lips tighten to stop me from saying something I will later regret.

"I've travelled all this way, the least you can do is acknowledge me."

I fold my arms across my chest. "You took the elevator to the roof and climbed into the helicopter. It's not exactly a bicycle ride from Scotland."

He grits his teeth. "My patience is growing thin."

"Mine too."

He's about to say something more when he notices we aren't alone. The wrinkle next to his eye twitches ever so slightly. Most people would probably miss it, but I know his tells. This is my father for you; he thinks about himself and our theme park first. It won't look good on him to continue this conversation around the wrong people, even if they are just children. His brooding eyes give me a stern stare, silently telling me I've won the battle, but he's claiming victory on the war.

As I turn away from him, I notice my mistake. A new crowd has formed behind me. My plan for staying under the radar is blown out of the water. Not that it matters now. The parents stay together; their curiosity shines like a beacon I'd like to avoid. I dismiss the group, making my way over to Kara, who's standing with Hayley and Anna. We've only spoken a few times, but after getting a glimpse into her opinion of me, I still want her to believe I'm the carefree skateboarder she suggested I was. Maybe I can play this down.

"Is that your dad?" she asks.

Or maybe not.

I offer a small hand flip in acknowledgement. My dad's on the Forbes' billionaires list. With a quick internet search, it wouldn't be hard to work out who I am. Graham Oaks is a successful businessman, who regularly features in magazines and on television. Hell, I'm all over the Blue Oaks website if you look close enough. People don't always recognise me straight away, but when they see us together, it's obvious he's my dad. His chiselled features reflect my own. Other than the silvery grey hair and deep-set lines he has, I'm his double. With a few pieces of the puzzle revealed, I'm no longer just some skateboarder. I'm the sole heir to a multi-million pound estate.

Kara's attention stays with my father as she directs her words at me. "If you need anything, don't hesitate to ask."

Not many people would offer me assistance. They presume my life is too easy to need help. I can't hide the surprise on my face. The corners of my lips turn up in gratitude. Kara doesn't treat me like some spoiled rich boy. Instead, she shows empathy. She puts her arms around Hayley and Anna, leading them to their car. She glances back at me one last time before disappearing out of sight.

Once the last of the group leaves, Aaron comes to stand next to me. My focus stays on the surrounding scenery.

"Do you want me to help you get out of here?"

"No. I can handle this. You go ahead, and I'll see you back at the hostel."

He pats me on the back before starting to pack the van. Time stands still while I wait for him to leave. The tap of the cane and shuffle of gravel lets me know my father is approaching.

"Let's go have dinner."

I look down at my washed-out cargo shorts, offering my dad a shrug. The sort of place he will have in mind comes with a dress code. One I don't fit. He would rather go hungry than eat at a fast food joint which doesn't leave us with many options.

"I'll have Floyd phone ahead and arrange a table in the back of the restaurant."

I roll my eyes. At least he didn't suggest hiring me a suit. An estate car pulls into the nearby car park. My father walks over to it and doesn't look back. I've already given up my chance to escape, so after a deep breath, I set my feet into motion to join him.

My dad wasn't joking when he said a seat in the back. The curtain is drawn around our table as I focus on the Italian menu. The waiter fills my glass with mineral water and makes a swift exit. My dad hasn't spoken to me since we left the youth centre. I study the menu for a few more minutes.

"I'll return home at the end of the summer," I say.

"That's not the deal I agreed to, Julian." His eyes stay on the menu.

"What difference will a couple of months make? I'm doing everything you ask."

"This isn't open to negotiations. I gave you what you wanted, and you still ran. It's time to start being responsible."

"I just can't do it, Dad. The social dinners and the same faux people are just too much. I don't want that life." The distaste seeps from my voice and I can't hide it.

"Forget the dinners. I'm not forcing you to attend any charity balls. Just come home."

The waiter interrupts our conversation by clearing his throat. He takes our order, leaving a basket of freshly made bread. The candle flickers as the curtain closes behind him. He's not the only one who wishes he could escape this room quickly.

"I'm not you. I have no intention of finding a girl to settle down with. You know I love working in the theme park, but I don't want the rest of the hassle. I want my own life."

"I'm not forcing you to do anything."

"If that's the case, I'll stay on the urban circuit for the summer, and you can stop harassing Aaron."

We sit in silence until the waiter brings our food. The smell instantly makes my mouth water. My diet on the road would give my dad another reason to hate my choice in life. I know he only wants the best for me, but his judgement is clouded by his own ambition. We don't usually fight. It's just the two of us, and he needs me as much as I need him, but having my future set in stone by someone else is a difficult thing to swallow.

CHAPTER TEN

KARA

Seeing Bear with his dad struck a nerve. Parental issues are something I'm familiar with. The scowl on his face told me everything I needed to know. The offer to help slipped from my lips before I could think it through. I don't know his situation, yet I felt an overwhelming obligation to let him know he has options, even if it's only someone to talk to.

The girls follow me into the house, looking at their mobile phones. I'm the first to catch sight of my sister, and her guilty look has me narrowing my eyes.

"It isn't what it looks like," Helen says, holding her hands up, letting the chocolate wrapper fall between the cushions.

The girls push me out of the way as they barrel into the house. A re-run of *Friends* is playing on the television. My sister stays frozen to the spot, waiting to see if I'll tell them her secret. The girls are too giddy from their exciting day to notice Helen's suspicious behaviour.

"Call us when tea is ready. We'll be in our room," Anna says.

They disappear up the stairs, stomping every step of the way. Helen and I stare at each other for a few seconds longer, making sure the girls are out of hearing range.

"I hope you've saved some of them for me," I say, licking my lips.

Unzipping my thin summer coat, I hang it on a peg and slip my shoes onto the shelf below it as Helen waves a small bar of chocolate at me. I join her on the sofa. Strawberry creams are our favourites. I bet she's been saving these for a sneaky treat. Helen likes to set the girls a good example and she wouldn't want to be caught snacking before tea. Without an ounce of guilt for not sharing with Anna and Hayley, I rip open the wrapper. The chocolate melts in my mouth, releasing the strawberry cream as my taste buds dance with delight.

"You're home early." It's only four p.m., and usually, Helen works later.

"Derrick asked me to visit some office space with him."

"Where is he?"

"He's signing the paperwork. It looks like he's serious about moving back to town, at least for now.

Are you up for peeling some carrots while I prepare the chicken?"

Derrick's decision to rent office space explains why my sister is comfort eating. Helen offers me a hand up from the sofa. We race into the kitchen like children, laughing as we fight over the kitchen counter. Pushing the chopping board onto the side, I beat her to her usual spot. She rubs her hands together, signalling she has a plan. My eyes narrow in anticipation. She gets the chicken from the fridge and places a strawberry cream on the furthest edge of the table. It's a trick and I know it, yet that doesn't mean I can resist. The chocolate is worth giving up my position. Making a beeline for the table, I grab the chocolate bar like it's the last one of its kind. Helen claims her usual work station with a glint of satisfaction in her eyes. I move the bin to the table, setting up with the peeler in hand and resting my foot on a chair.

"So, what's going on with Derrick?"

"He says he made a mistake and wants his family back. Not just the girls. He wants us to give our relationship another try."

"Why now?"

"He's forty in a couple of weeks. I think he's having a midlife crisis."

My lips curl up into a forced smile. It's difficult to know what to think. When they split up, it was because Derrick worked away a lot. Even if he moves his office back here, he will still need to travel. Placing the sliced carrot into the steamer, I grab another.

"Toby's leaving for a job at the theme park," I say, trying to hide the sadness in my voice.

"And I suppose you're staying here?"

"Of course."

"When does he leave?"

"Tomorrow."

"So soon."

"I think he was scared to tell me."

She gives me a look which I've seen plenty of times before. My sister thinks Toby puts himself first too often.

Turning the timer, I set the steamer to cook the vegetables. Helen puts the meat in the oven. We settle back on the sofa as the front door opens and Derrick appears in the hallway. He pauses when he sees us. The next twenty minutes are painful as we sit in silence, watching TV. I'd excuse myself if it wasn't for Helen giving me the evil eye.

The bell rings on the steamer, saving me. I shoot off the sofa faster than an Olympic runner. Armed with oven gloves, I serve up the chicken and vegetables while Helen shouts for the girls to come downstairs.

"How was the summer club?" Derrick asks as we settle at the kitchen table.

"We've met so many cool people. I wish it wasn't ending," Hayley says.

"High school is going to be a blast. There are loads of after school clubs I want to join," Anna adds.

A smile creeps onto my face. I'm happy for the girls. Even if they want different things, I know they will stay close. Thinking of my best friend leaving tomorrow weakens my smile. We're usually joined at the hip. A strange feeling settles in my chest. My summer plan for two has become a pity party for one.

"Why is the club ending?" Derrick asks.

"They're moving on to another town. Some of the kids are going to a swimming club but it's expensive."

"I'll cover the cost," he says.

Helen glares at him. My heart sinks further realising the girls won't be spending their full days with me. Hayley and Anna give a cheer while Derrick struggles to control his satisfied smile. I can feel a storm is brewing. I'm hoping we can make it through the meal without any arguments, but Helen looks less than impressed. Luckily, the tension goes straight over the girls' heads.

Anna hands out butterfly buns as I make cups of tea. Helen washes the dishes, keeping her thoughts to herself. She thrusts the dirty plates into the sink and bangs them on the draining board. Taking my cup of tea with me, I make an excuse to leave Helen and Derrick to resolve their issues in private. The girls race into the living room to call dibs on the television. Derrick's raised voice echoes around the kitchen as I mount the stairs. I find a movie to watch, settling into bed for the night.

Hours later, the door clicking shut wakes me from my sleep. The room is almost black, but I would recognise Helen's footsteps anywhere. She creeps into the room, walking straight into the metal bed frame. She hops on one foot, cursing under her breath. I turn over to face her, pulling the covers back for her to get in.

"Sorry if I woke you."

"I hope your toe isn't broken."

"It's just a bump."

She hobbles around the room, looking for her pyjamas. Turning the lamp on, I cover my head with the duvet. A few moments later, her side of the bed dips down as she climbs in. She leans across me to turn off the light. Lifting the covers off my head, I find Helen on the edge of her pillow, staring at me.

"What did Derrick have to say?"

"Who the hell knows what's going on in his head? He's trying to fit back into our lives, but I'm not sure how it's going to work." She lets out a sigh before she continues. "Don't worry about me. How are you feeling about Toby leaving tomorrow?"

"I'll admit it's strange to think he'll be gone, but it will give me more family time. I'm looking forward to having popcorn and movie nights."

"I'm going to miss you when you leave. The way you help with the girls is more than I could ever ask for. You've been amazing. It doesn't matter if you leave tomorrow or in September, you have to know I'm grateful for everything, but we will be fine without you."

"I love you," I say.

"I love you too."

Helen lets out a few deep sighs, like more words are playing on the tip of her tongue. She seems to be struggling to get them out. My eyes feel heavy, and even though I want to stay awake, it isn't long until I drift off. Tomorrow is another day, and whatever Helen has on her mind can wait.

CHAPTER ELEVEN

KARA

Dropping the girls at the summer club left me with time to myself. I haven't heard from Toby, even though he's leaving in just over an hour. I already feel like I've been forgotten. Silence rings through the house as the door clicks behind me. My body relaxes against the wooden panels as my head presses against the frosted glass. I reach into my pocket and pull out my phone with the intention of playing some music.

A notification thanking me for my application to Blue Oaks displays on the screen. I run my hands through my hair. There must be some kind of mistake. Instead of opening the email, I ignore it and return to my first thought. After choosing an up-beat playlist, I make my way into the kitchen. Flicking the kettle on, I dance around the room, preparing my mug. A bright yellow notelet in the centre of the table catches my eye, making me do a double take.

The orange shiny tickets stop my breath as I read Helen's handwriting on the note.

Good luck.

I slowly take a seat at the table, staring at the tickets to Blue Oaks train station. Feeling overwhelmed, I can't help but smile which I cover with my hand. Excitement flutters through my core. Checking the time on my phone, I shoot out of my seat. I have to get going if I want to do this.

I run upstairs and pull out my suitcase from under the bed in the office, frantically packing everything that fits in. Once it's bursting at the seams, I sit on top of it to squash it down, trying to fasten the zip.

I push the suitcase to the top of the stairs before I realise it's too heavy. Something has to give. The zip slides undone with a tug. I get rid of the books and most of my shoes before closing the case back up. With a lighter load, it's easier to drag it downstairs. I quickly move to the front door to put on my coat. I'm out of breath and take a second to gather my thoughts. Can I really do this?

I find my abandoned phone in the kitchen and dial Toby's number. It feels like minutes rather than seconds while I wait for him to answer. It rings until it goes to voicemail. I stare at my phone for a few seconds until I realise he isn't going to call me back. My fingers search for the Blue Oaks email and find the job offer. The one I didn't apply for but successfully got. I call Toby a few more times which ends in the same result. He isn't answering.

My best friend leaves in less than twenty minutes. It's now or never if I want to catch the train. The Uber app helps me schedule a taxi, and I wait outside for it to arrive. Butterflies flutter in my stomach as the car pulls up. The driver helps me with my suitcase and I climb in to the back of the car with my ticket in hand.

The ride to the station is a blur and my heart races with excitement and nerves. I stare out of the window, unable to take in the familiar surroundings. The driver turns to face me. It's then I notice we've stopped moving. I blink at him a couple of times before coming back to my senses.

"We're here. You can get out now and I'll help you with your bag." His rough voice makes me jump.

I blink a couple of times before I shake my head and exit the vehicle. I stand on the side of the road, my eyes wide, taking in the small station. A text message from Helen snaps me out of my daze. *Go have fun,* it reads, with a smiley face on the end. Slowly, I walk onto the empty platform. My heart sinks when I realise Toby is nowhere in sight. I let my case drop to the floor and sit on the cold metal bench.

A few seconds later a voice behind me says, "I thought you weren't coming."

The corners of my mouth instantly lift into a

bright smile. Turning around, I see Toby with a paper cup in his hand and a rucksack on his back. Chewing on his bottom lip, he comes to stand in front of me.

"The train is due in a few minutes," he says. "Do you want me to grab you a hot drink?"

"I can get one on the train."

He swings his arms in a happy jig as a broad smile spreads across his face. "I'm glad you came. We're going to have an awesome time."

I twist my hair around my fingers. Looking out onto the tracks, the train slowly rolls closer until it stops in the station.

"Are you ready?"

Toby is waiting for me to fully commit. He holds his breath with a serious expression on his face.

"Let's do this."

I hold my hand up high and Toby meets it with his palm. A celebratory high-five is all the confirmation he needs. There is a giddiness to his step as we get on the train.

Once we find our seats, I message Helen to tell her I made it to the station. As I begin to feel comfortable, questions start to run through my mind.

"Who filled in my application for Blue Oaks?"

"Sorry not sorry. I'm guilty, your honour."

I bite my nail. "Did you arrange accommodation?"

"Sit back, relax, and enjoy the ride. Everything is under control. Here, take my drink and I'll go find another."

The alert for the doors closing signals the train is about to set off. An announcement plays through the overhead speaker telling us about our journey. Toby disappears down the train as I bring the paper cup to my lips and watch my hometown slip away into the background.

CHAPTER TWELVE

BEAR

I haven't spoken to my dad since he left last night. After our meal, we went for a walk along the River Tyne. Our conversation stayed light, even though I could see his frustration. My dad wants me to come home, but I'm not ready yet. He didn't push for a fight and we left things on good terms.

I spend the evening posting leaflets and talking to a few guys in the local skate park. When I reach the hostel, there's a note from Aaron pinned to the door. It tells me he left the key to our room with the cleaner who lives on site. Once I have access to the room, it doesn't take me long to work out that Aaron left in a rush. His paperwork for the charity accounts are sprawled out on his bed. My eyes wander across the negative numbers on the pages. This is worse than I thought. A few van repairs and equipment replacement soon adds up. I rest my knee on the end of his bed, trying to take in the new information. The handle to the door begins to turn as I pick up the latest bill. Aaron pauses in the threshold. His shoulders slump forward as a frown appears on his face.

"Sorry, Bear. I didn't mean for you to see this. I had a last minute meeting and forgot to move them."

"You should've told me how bad it is. I could have..."

"Don't ask your dad for help. I don't want you to do that."

My hands tighten into fists. "I started this journey to offer you support. I like being on the road with you, but the best way I can help is to go home."

I start to pace the room. My mind is made up; going home isn't what I want, but I need to fix this the only way I know how. Staying here is putting us both at a disadvantage. There will be no charity if Aaron can't boost the funds and I'm in a position to get the donations needed to keep the charity going. It's the right thing to do. This is the push I need to put my future back on track. Avoiding my responsibilities is something I'm good at, and if I'm honest with myself, going home scares me. That's why I fought it. I don't want to fail. The family business is my calling and I'm frightened I won't be able to make my dad proud. Aaron shakes his head, though I can see the relief in his eyes. His reaction finalises my decision. Using Aaron's laptop, I buy a ticket for the first train tomorrow morning, and then I call my dad. He answers his phone on the first ring.

"What are your demands?"

Am I really that predictable?

Aaron rubs his hands over his face as I speak.

"You know about the lack of funds for the sports programme. But how..."

"It's my job to know everything about my son."

He spends too much time concentrating on what I'm doing and what's happening in the park. I'd suggest he found a hobby or a girlfriend, but he's not interested in either. It's like his whole life is dedicated to the family estate. Since Mum died, he won't do anything other than work, and I'm okay with that. I just wish he could understand me a little more.

"I want you to donate a year's worth of funding, including school visits, and a bonus for Aaron's hard work."

"Done."

It's settled then. I can get Aaron what he needs and my dad gets what he wants.

"I'll be home tomorrow."

"It's about time. I've missed you."

"I've missed you, too. I don't want to fight anymore."

"It's only because I care."

"See you soon. Goodbye."

"Goodbye."

Ending the call, I toss the phone on the bed.

Aaron is about to start protesting again, so I hold up my hand to stop him. Summer dreams of helping the children and getting to know a cute girl evaporates. I want to try and forget my freedom has been cut short. Blue Oaks is where I belong, and at least this way, I can save the charity. I don't want my dad to think I'm not interested in the park because it's not true; I just don't want to disappoint anyone. I can no longer put off my future, but at least I'm going home on my terms.

CHAPTER THIRTEEN

KARA

Studying the cartoon-style map, I search for the swan ride. The uniform moves in the opposite direction of my skin. It feels hard, crisp, and uncomfortable, like I'm wearing a paper bag. I try not to pull my shirt down for the tenth time. I left Toby at the edge of the park, and he set off in the opposite direction. My late application meant I had to take a job in a different zone of the theme park to him.

My gaze glides across the beautiful lake. The trees outline the edge, making it feel tranquil rather than part of a noisy theme park. On the opposite side of the water is the place I'm supposed to be. I focus on the ripples, trying to calm my nerves. The ducks are the only ones using the lake right now.

I take a step back from between the trees, not looking where I'm going. A guy's voice yelps as something sharp hits my ankle, knocking me off balance. Strong arms wrap around my shoulders, but it isn't enough. Before I know what's happening, the ice cold water surrounds me and I'm gasping for air. My hands shoot out, searching for anything to grab onto. Panic begins to set in as I kick my limbs in all directions, desperate to find a lifeline. A hand yanks me out of the lake, laying me on the ground. I cough up the water lodged in my throat while trying to ease the tightening in my chest. Water is dripping down my face, hair, and new uniform.

"What the hell were you doing? How did you not hear me coming? Now we're both going to be late. You need to watch where you're going."

"I'm sorry. It was an accident. It's my first day and I was trying to navigate the map."

Wiping the water out of my eyes, I turn to face my victim. Even soaked to the bone, I know it's him. My breath catches in my throat for a whole new reason. It's Bear.

The pieces begin to fit into place. I *knew* he looked familiar. He's the model from the newspaper. His brown hair and eyes are unmistakable. His wet clothes outline his toned body. Instead of grovelling for forgiveness, I eye him up like a piece of juicy steak. Bear is beautiful, even submerged in dirty lake water. Toby was right; this park really does support skilled workers.

"You're the inspirational talent."

"What?"

I didn't mean to say that out loud, and I shake my head. "Never mind."

His eyebrows squeeze together in confusion, and a sour grin crosses his lips. He shakes his head, rubbing the excess water from his hair. "Are you following me?"

The words feel like an accusation. The kindness in his eyes is missing. My mouth falls open while I try to figure out if he's being serious.

"How would I know you'd be here?"

His face tightens into a grimace. "You met my dad. I thought... You know what, it doesn't matter. I don't have time for this. I never expected a glimpse of my lost freedom to follow me here."

Offering me a hand up, he pulls me to my feet. Without looking back at me, he picks up his skateboard, leaving me to watch him disappear. I have no idea if he's upset with me or just needs some time to cool off. It's not like I intended for us to fall in the lake. It was an accident. I'm not usually so clumsy. I'm just on edge because it's my first day away from my family. He was nice at the summer club. His first impression of me is the one I want him to remember, not the rambling girl he just encountered. He probably hates me now and is going to tell all his friends about the girl who ruined his morning.

Awesome. Way to go, Kara!

It's official. I'm going to be late on my first day. Lucky for me, I have a week's worth of uniforms in my locker. I quickly hurry to change my clothes while ignoring the funny looks from anyone who passes me by. There's nothing I can do about my hair, but at least I won't be putting the customers off by dripping water everywhere.

The door to the changing room swings open and a thirty-something-year-old dressed as a fairy godmother enters. She stops mid-step when she sees me. Her hands cover her mouth as she lets out a gasp.

"What happened to you?" she asks.

I look worse than I thought.

She pushes her silver sparkly glasses up her nose to take a closer look. Her hand moves to a poised fairy position, as if her character is second nature.

"I took the scenic route. I don't suppose you can work your magic on my hair?"

"Honey, no amount of magic can fix that. You need a shower. I can help with your shoe problem though."

She opens her locker. Inside is every colour of the rainbow. Glitter and pom-poms are bursting from the seams. There isn't a hint of black anywhere.

"What size do you wear?"

"Five. Thank you."

She passes me a pair of ruby red pixie style shoes. They go against the dress code, but what choice do I have? Plus, aren't rules meant to be broken, especially when this adventure is supposed to be fun? My first day can't get any worse, so I have nothing to lose. I thank the fairy godmother again and hurry out of the changing rooms.

When I reach the large swan pedal boats, my heart is beating fast and my knees feel weak. Relying on Toby has become second nature to me. I'm on my own for now, and showing I can do this is a step closer to an independent future. I sweep my wet hair up into a bun and run lip balm over my dry lips. While looking around for the person who is going to show me the ropes, my eyes lock with Bear's. In the newspaper, it said his name was Julian, but his badge only offers his nickname. I knew that couldn't be the name written on his birth certificate. Under his name on the identification badge is the job title: Senior Management. Holy hell, I'm going to get fired before I've even begun. I cup my hands over my mouth and suck in a deep breath. The blink of my eyes kicks into overdrive, and he probably thinks I'm about to pass out.

Shaking my head, I clear the negative thoughts before plastering a fake smile on my face. Instead of mentioning our previous meetings, I introduce myself.

"I'm your newest starter, Kara."

"Here I was thinking I'd imagined seeing you this morning."

"No, it's me in the flesh, and I'm ready to knuckle down and learn all about the theme park."

My cheekbones are too high as I try to sweeten my smile.

A groan rumbles from his chest, and he turns to leave me watching him walk away for the second time today. I trip on the decking as my feet set in motion to follow him. I'm literally falling out of step today and I need to get a grip on my new situation.

"First rule is to watch where you're going. We don't want anyone to fall into the lake. Do you know what an emergency stop button looks like?"

"Big and red?"

Bear turns to look at my shoes and my cheeks warm. He rolls his eyes, continuing on his path to the control room. Stumbling along, I follow like an obedient employee. Once inside, he palms his wet hair, flattening it to his head.

"Sit here and watch the monitors. If someone starts messing around, press the green button on the microphone and tell them to take a seat. Do you think you can handle that?"

"Yes, but..."

He doesn't give me a chance to finish as he rushes out the door leaving me staring at the place he once stood. The room is small and basic. Drumming my fingers against my side, I glance at the television monitor. The picture of the lake is grainy and doesn't do it any justice. This is not what I had in mind. My day isn't going as planned and this doesn't scream *summer of fun*. Actually, it feels more like I should turn and run.

Untamed curly hair is only going to do one thing when it dries and by lunchtime, I look like I should be in the Stone Age part of the park. Brushing my fingers through the tangled mess, I try to take back some control. Scraping it back into a bun, I stretch my hair tie over my hair. The sharp snap of the elastic twanging against my hand lets me know my bad luck isn't over yet. With a heavy sigh, I turn back to my task. My hair is the least of my worries at this moment. Finding a way to beat the boredom and stay awake is more important.

Toby is too busy to meet me for lunch, so I end up sitting alone on the secluded banking. It would've been nice to see him, but I'm also glad to have some time to myself. My afternoon is as unremarkable as the morning, watching Bear handle the whole ride while he makes me sit in the control room. My eyes are heavy by the time the shift ends.

The door opening startles me, and I sit up a little straighter. Bear stares right at me, pointing in my direction.

"It's time to go home, water girl."

His stern mood appears to have relaxed a little. He doesn't smile, but at least he's not frowning at me anymore. Jumping off the seat, I follow him out the door. An apology is playing on my lips, but the words are stuck in my throat. All I want to do is climb into bed and start a fresh day tomorrow.

CHAPTER FOURTEEN

KARA

When I arrive back at our camping pod, the place is in darkness; Toby isn't back yet. I take the stairs two at a time, and hop onto the deck. I'm feeling instantly better now I've escaped my horrible first day at work. The key fits into the lock with ease and I open the door. My finger flicks the light switch on and I grab a towel from under my camp bed. My hair looks like straw when I finally look in the mirror. Luckily, I'm not the type of girl who worries about her appearance.

The hot, steamy water feels amazing as it glides down my body. I use half a bottle of strawberry shower gel to make sure I've got rid of all the dirty water. Once I'm squeaky clean, I return to the pod. The place still looks desolate and it's so small you wouldn't miss a bug moving across the floor.

Switching the kettle on, I pick up my phone to call home. Anna answers on the first ring.

"How did your first day go? Tell me everything and don't spare me any of the details."

I can't tell her I've upset her skateboard instructor. Both girls think he's great, and I'm embarrassed thinking about what happened today. Before I get a chance to say a word, there's a high-pitched scream and a rustling sound. My face screws up, trying to block out the noise. A few seconds later, a video call alert pops up on my phone. The girls appear side by side on the bed, smiling sweetly. Helen's head is poking around in the background.

"Operation best summer ever has begun," I say with a nervous laugh.

A shadow creeps up behind me and my pulse quickens. I jump out of my skin as Toby's grey, peeling face comes in to view. His arms brush over my shoulders as he makes zombie noises.

"Holy hell, you scared the life out of me. I thought you were supposed to get changed before you left the park."

He breaks character, laughing at my reaction.

"Sophie offered to show me a shortcut and I didn't want to keep her waiting."

Peering over my shoulder, Toby waves to my family. His costume smells like it's over a hundred years old. The fabric looks like it's covered in cement or thick clay. It has the same starched look as my uniform, there's nothing that will soften its edges.

"Hey, everyone. I'm sure Kara's already told you, but this place is fantastic. Today's the start of the summer fun. Scaring dads who have taken their kids into the spooky house is hilarious." He laughs.

I offer a weak smile. "It sounds like Toby had fun today. Anyway, enough about Blue Oaks, how are you guys doing?"

"We're going to watch a movie and Dad's cooking tonight," Anna says.

"Aw, I'm missing out."

"You're spending your time at a theme park. I bet you've already had donuts. We're the ones missing out," Hayley says.

I shake my head. "No sugary treats yet but I'll have an extra one for you when I do."

Anna screws up her face. We talk a little more before we say our goodbyes. Waving, I click the end call button on the phone. As soon as the line goes dead, Toby studies me with an intense look.

"Okay, spill. What's wrong? How did your day go?"

Toby can read me so well; there's no point in denying it. I fill him in with the details of my terrible day while he laughs hysterically.

"It isn't that funny." I try to stop a smile forming on my face.

"Is there a video? That has to be worth two

hundred and fifty pounds if we send it in to *You've Been Framed*."

I purse my lips. "This is like the first day of Year Seven all over again, when I accidentally made Holly Olsen face plant into her yoghurt."

He laughs even harder, holding his stomach. I was scarred for life after that day in school. She spent the next month making my life hell and it was a total accident.

Okay, so maybe I'm clumsy when I'm nervous, or just unlucky. Shaking the memory away, I try to focus on today's mistake.

"Who the hell rides a skateboard down a public path anyway?" I ask.

"The guy you dragged into the lake, that's who."

"Shut up." I swat him with my pillow.

"Let's go out for tea to cheer you up. I'll get a shower, and then I'm all yours."

Toby is quick even for a guy. He has jeans and a plain t-shirt on before I can put my shoes on.

It's only a short walk to the Frog and Goat pub which is located just outside the theme park's main gates. Finding a table in one of the pub alcoves, I take a seat, while Toby goes to the bar. A familiar face appears at my side, though I can't place her straight away.

"How did the rest of your day go?"

Her eyes twinkle as her kind smile lights up.

"Fairy godmother?"

Her fairy-tale laugh fills the air. "My friends call me Lynne." She winks at me, causing my own smile to mirror hers.

"Nobody else fell in the lake, so that has to count for something. Let's hope my victim doesn't hold a lifetime grudge." I cross my fingers, holding them up in the air.

"I'm sure it was an accident and it won't happen again. You can turn it around. We'll make a star out of you yet."

"I'll be lucky to last the week. I think my new boss hates me. One more mistake and I'll be on the first train home."

The door to the Frog and Goat pub opens. I would recognise that confident, masculine walk anywhere. He has an aura about him that grabs the attention of everyone in the room. His broad shoulders sway as he makes his way to the bar. I try to keep my head down, hoping he doesn't see me.

"Oh, hell. He just walked in."

Bear joins a group of people around the fireplace. He greets them like he hasn't seen them in years, hugging each one in turn. My nose wrinkles in confusion. What makes him so special?

"You know who that is, right?"

"He's the poster boy. The talent. The park eye candy."

She laughs again with a hint of mischief in her eyes. She's waiting for something I don't have and I wonder if the helicopter is more significant than I realised. I've never travelled by air before. Could Bear's dad be rich or something? Her smile deepens when she realises I don't know the answer.

"This could get interesting," she says, with a smirk on her face.

I try to ask her for the missing piece, but she puts her finger to her lips, signalling the secret is locked away. Bear said something about his dad this morning. If Lynne doesn't want to tell me, I can wait until someone does. Toby brings two pints of beer to the table, placing them on the cardboard mats.

"I took the liberty of ordering you a cheeseburger with chips. Who's your friend?"

"This is Lynne, my personal fairy godmother. I'm Kara, and this is my good friend Toby."

"Welcome to Blue Oaks, the place where dreams come true." She sings the words in her character voice. She waves goodbye when she sees her own friend returning from the bar.

"See, I knew your day couldn't have been that bad. You've made a new friend."

"She took pity on me after my dip in the lake."

He laughs. "So you've made a friend for life."

I take a drink of my beer. "Tell me about your day. Is perfect Sophie everything she claimed to be?"

A loud howl of laughter echoes through the pub. Bear's arms are flying in all directions while he tells what I imagine is a dramatic story. He has a beautiful smile. I shouldn't be thinking about his lips, yet I struggle to look away. His eyes fill with animation over his story. When his gaze casts over me, a scowl instantly appears. Quickly, I turn away to find Toby studying me.

"I'm sorry," I say. "What?"

"Sophie. I knew you weren't listening. You were too busy drooling over Mr. Big Shot over there."

"I was not doing anything of the sort."

Toby rolls his eyes. "Sophie is great, though I'm not sure I have a chance of being anything other than a friend." He shrugs as if he isn't bothered, although I know him better than that.

"Why? What's wrong?"

"She's a free spirit. She doesn't believe in commitment."

A smile creeps onto my face. "Maybe you've met your match." I take another drink of my beer.

"He's still looking over here. I think it's you who's in trouble."

This is one of those moments where I wish I could slide down into my chair and hide.

"He's probably planning his revenge. That's the guy I put in the lake."

I lower my head to try and hide my embarrassment as Toby laughs hysterically.

The waitress arrives with our food. She puts the plates, a handful of sauce sachets, and cutlery on the table. Toby takes a big bite of his burger as I thank the waitress. The whole time I'm eating, I feel Bear's eyes burning into the back of my skull. It's either that, or I'm getting paranoid. Either way, I keep my concentration on my food and fight the urge to look in his direction.

CHAPTER FIFTEEN

BEAR

Today was unusual for Blue Oaks theme park. Kara Edwards is someone I never expected to see again and it set my whole day in a spin. If I hadn't been so shocked by the cold water, I might've reacted differently to her.

I watch her from across the bar, my second pint going down easier than the first. The universe is punishing me for giving in to my dad's demands, and whatever set my karma off balance is working overtime. I should be grateful; at least my summer just got interesting in a different way, but I feel out of sorts. My focus is blurring and I promised myself the park would have my full attention when I returned. Kara spiked my interest the second I met her back in Northumberland, but I didn't want her to cross into my world. I'm no longer just a carefree skater boy, and it won't be long before she finds out who I am. If she hasn't already. It's myself I'm annoyed with. She was the one person I wanted to believe the illusion; to think I was just like everyone else. I didn't want to be back here just yet, and seeing her put me on edge. I don't need the extra stress. I should have played nice with her, but I let my temper get the better of me.

It's not all on me though. We ended up in the lake because of her. Seeing her sitting in the corner of the pub means she isn't going to quit, which means she's going to be a constant reminder of the freedom I've given up. The determination on her face when she turned up in those glittery pixie shoes made it difficult to be mad at her, and I wasn't really. I didn't want her to catch a cold, so I did the only thing I could. By putting her in the control room, it gave me a chance to calm down and her time to dry off. When I left Northumberland, I thought I was closing a chapter on my life and putting my serious head on. Now I'm conflicted about wanting to be professional for the park and getting to know Kara. I didn't want my personal life and the park to become one and the same. I wanted more time to enjoy myself before I had to start putting the family business first.

Mike, my friend who works on the runaway train ride, nudges me to bring me back to the conversation.

"Sorry, guys. I'm just tired. It's been a crazy week. What did I miss?"

He tilts his head towards Kara. "Who's the girl?"

"She's a new recruit," I say nonchalantly.

"Are you into her?"

A goofy grin plays on his face. Pointing at him, I try to take a serious stance. "Leave her alone."

He throws his head back and laughs. Chloe and Vinnie, my other co-workers and long-term friends, smirk while I shrug it off.

"If that girl over there helps you stay at my side, I'll take it," Vinnie says. He usually works with me on the swan ride, but today was his day off.

"It's missing your ugly face that got me to come home."

Vinnie likes to pretend he isn't vain, yet grooming his dark brown beard is something he takes pride in. He knows he's good-looking.

"I knew it. You can't stay away from me."

He is the only person who knows I'm nervous about my future. We keep our conversations light, but he was the only person I discussed leaving for the summer with. He's a good friend, even if he doesn't always agree with my choices.

Lynne winks at me as she walks across the room to the bar. Finishing my last mouthful of beer, I join her, leaning against the varnished wood. When she sees me standing next to her, she leans in close.

"A little bird told me you went for a swim this morning," she says.

"From that information, I'm guessing you've made a new friend."

My gaze drifts over to Kara. The change in angle allows me to see the guy she's with. He's probably her boyfriend. A scowl forms on my face. I shouldn't care. This girl isn't for me.

"Kara's a nice girl, so don't be too hard on her. It was her first day. I've got to ask though... how did you both fall in the lake?"

I wave Lynne off. "I've blocked the whole thing from my memory."

"What can I get you, Lynne?" Jim asks as he approaches us from behind the bar.

Blue Oaks is a small community, and everyone knows just about everybody. The local people are like a big family. They look out for each other.

"I'll get these. I'll have a beer and a..." I say, pausing for Lynne to fill in the blank.

"My usual, please, Jim. White wine spritzer."

"What can you tell me about the new girl?" I ask Lynne, trying to sound indifferent.

"Didn't you spend the day with her?" She tilts her head to the side, studying me. I shouldn't have asked but I couldn't hold my tongue. I want to know more about Kara.

"She pulled me into the lake. I haven't exactly been the best company." I give a little shrug, trying to downplay my reaction.

"Other than her shoe size, I don't know much. I can take her off your hands if you'd like. She's a pretty little thing and would make a cute fairy."

My Kara problem would be solved if I let her work with Lynne. I wouldn't have to see her. Yet, I can't bring myself to let her go.

Instead, I ignore her question and my attention drifts to Jim placing our drinks on the beer mats. I reach into my pocket, pulling out a handful of change to pay the bill. Once I have my pint, I go back to my friends, leaving Lynne talking to Jim.

"What did I miss?" I take a sip of my beer.

"You could've got me another one," Vinnie says, shaking his empty glass.

Usually I would have bought him a drink. This is another sign I'm distracted.

"Sorry. Next round I will."

"You won't be making it in to work tomorrow if you keep this up," Chloe says.

She's a petite blonde who can't handle more than two glasses of wine. I shrug off her comment, knowing there's more chance of her being hung-over tomorrow.

"We're thinking of inviting the newbies to our capture the flag game tomorrow. What do you think?" Mike asks me.

My gaze flickers to Kara. "The more the merrier."

———

When I arrive home, my dad's in the hallway on the phone, talking to a business associate. His face remains expressionless as I catch his eye.

"I'm sorry. I'll call you back."

He holds up his hand, signalling for me to wait while he rounds up his call. Once he's finished, he turns to talk to me.

I let out a sigh, waiting for the lecture.

"Did you have a good night with your friends?"

"Yes, they're glad I'm back."

"So am I."

"Great."

My tone holds a little bitterness which I can't completely hide. I like being with my friends here but I don't share their enthusiasm for my return. I only wanted one last summer of freedom.

"The theme park isn't a punishment, Julian. It's a blessing. I never wanted you to feel like it was a burden. If you'd like to mix it up, why not swap your job into the offices or security? You can have any job you'd like."

I can't talk to my dad about why I've been avoiding the park. While I love it here, that's not the problem. My dad doesn't know what failure means. I'm scared I'll mess up and cost the park money, or its reputation. He's training me to take over the park someday, one step at a time. Ultimately, I'll become him one day. Mr Oaks, businessman extraordinaire, or so he thinks. It's a lot of pressure, especially when he's so good at it.

"I'm happy where I am. As you said, I need to start from the ground and work up."

I don't need him to hold my hand the whole way. Plus, my job is safe. I'm getting the hang of running the park zone and working the swan ride.

"I know you think I'm rushing you, but someday, the responsibility of the whole park will fall on your shoulders. I want you to be ready."

Hell, I'm not sure I'll ever be ready.

"Are you trying to tell me something?"

He shakes his head. "No, nothing like that. I just don't want to leave anything to chance. I sent Aaron the donation and a little extra."

I'm glad for the change in conversation topic. Although, I had no doubts he would keep his word.

"Thanks. You know how important the charity is to me."

"You can support as many good causes as you like, but you need to utilise your time here. Don't fight your future. Embrace it and take control. You're Julian Lewis Oaks, heir to Blue Oaks estate. Even the town bears our family name. You can do good things here if you put your mind to it." His voice is full of pride for our legacy.

I nod in acknowledgement. I've heard this speech a thousand times before and it doesn't ease my mind one bit. I know who I am, I always have. It's a difficult position to be in. I want to be a normal guy and worry about my university degree and girls. Instead, I'm spending the next three years studying for a business degree to help me learn how to run the park. Then my dad will give me even more responsibility.

Turning away from him, I race upstairs. Speeches are all good in theory. Working out how to make them fit into my life is a different story.

I send a quick text to Aaron to confirm he has the money. He replies instantly with his gratitude. A picture follows his message, showing some of the children and a new recruit.

I start a new group chat with my friends from the pub. We need everyone from our zone at the game tomorrow night, new and old. I'll contact Antony and arrange for us to go up against the dark woods team. The park is divided into zones and the dark woods team are our closest allies.

CHAPTER SIXTEEN

KARA

The light shimmers across the lake as dragonflies glide across the water. Taking a deep breath, I welcome the fresh new day. Yesterday's mistake is in the past. Today, my summer of fun begins. I've pressed the erase button on the whole disaster of the lake. Tucking my hair behind my ear, I step onto the main path. Bear flies down the hill on his skateboard, passing me with ease. A cluster of fairies laugh as they dance towards their castle. The park's enchanting music puts a spring in my step. My smile slides into place and I make my way around the lake.

I've got this.

The second my feet touch the deck of the ride's platform, my good mood wavers. Standing at the edge of the lake is Bear. His brown eyes never leave mine, like a crocodile waiting for its prey. I swallow down my nerves, taking a step closer. My tongue feels heavy and my palms itch as I approach him.

"Where are the leaves? You were rocking the swamp princess look."

He drums his foot against the floor. His frosty exterior from yesterday is replaced with amusement. Okay, so I can play his game.

"I thought I'd try something different today. You look good with your windswept skater hair. Did you decide to stay dry too?"

Oh, hell. Did I tell him he looks good? A flush of heat creeps up my face. Luckily, Bear doesn't seem to notice my mistake.

"I suggest staying out of the lake. Who knows what monster lurks in there. Are you sure you wouldn't be safer on the teacups?" His lip twitches.

"Actually, if you can reassign me, I'd like to be in the haunted house." I want to be with my best friend, but I'm not sure telling him that will help my case. I don't want him to think I'll avoid doing work just to hang out with Toby.

The playfulness in his face drops for a second, but he recovers quickly. "Your dream is to scare people? You should've stuck with the swamp look. Sorry, princess. No can do. My fortress is the enchanted forest. The haunted house belongs to the dark woods."

If only I could catch a bit of luck. You would think

a senior manager could pull some strings, but I guess not.

"Does the evil queen have you under her spell? You should find a frog to kiss to set you free of this enchanted forest."

He barks out a laugh. "You're not far off the mark. Instead of an evil queen, it's more along the lines of a mad king."

Who is the mad king? I haven't seen one of those around the enchanted forest. I rub the back of my neck. He might not be able to help me get a job with Toby, but there is something I want from him.

"Please don't lock me in the tower. I can't take another day in the control room."

I rub my elbow. Being shut in the small room for a day was bad enough. Even another hour would be too much.

"Yo, Vinnie. Are you up for taking some fresh meat off my hands?"

He shouts across the deck to a guy I recognise from the pub last night. I hold my breath, waiting for his answer. Do I want to be pawned off on someone else?

"No way, man. She's your problem."

He shakes his head while trying to suppress his smile.

Another laugh escapes Bear's lips. I have no idea what our conversation was really about, but I have a feeling it's something to do with his dad. Does it matter who he really is? Questioning him may not be the best move. I want him to like me. I need to get on his good side. At least until I can find my way into the dark woods. It doesn't matter how many dragons I need to slay; working with Toby is all I want.

"I won't be any trouble today," I say sweetly.

His big, brooding eyes burn into mine. He studies my face long enough for my nerves to kick back in. Tucking my hair behind my ear, I break eye contact to stare at my feet. The wet dew has stuck a small leaf to the edge of my shoe. Running my other foot over the leaf, it sweeps off. When I look back to Bear, he's already walking away.

"Let's start with a tour. The lake has been here as long as the house."

Pointing at the mansion, I say, "That's not a house."

He ignores my comment. "In the seventies, the gardens were open to the public and boats on the lake were one of the first attractions."

The history of the theme park is interesting, but I hope he doesn't quiz me on it. He seems to care about Blue Oaks and I'm not good at answering questions under pressure.

"When did you start working here?" I ask.

"I've always been part of the scenery. But, believe it or not, you're the first person I've ever pulled out of the lake."

He doesn't miss a beat to bring the conversation

full circle. I cringe. "I'm sorry about that." I bite my nail, hoping he will forgive me.

"Let's forget it. Just don't do it again."

He shakes off my words with the flick of his wrist. I nod enthusiastically.

"I'm ready to be the best team member you've got, or I'll settle for the least memorable."

I'm rambling again and I try not to fidget. He gets a lifejacket from one of the hooks and passes it to me.

"It's too late for that, princess. Today, you can help me assist people getting onto the swans. It's easy and hopefully will run smoothly."

Does his comment mean I've already messed up too much, or I've made an impression? I put the life-jacket on and fasten it into place.

"Have faith. I'm going to prove myself to you."

I'm not a klutz. I can handle this. I'm already less nervous than yesterday.

"I'm glad you said that. Tonight, we're holding a team-building drill. I expect you to be here on this deck by seven p.m."

"Yes, boss."

I salute him, which he ignores. My enthusiasm needs toning down a notch.

"The meeting is top secret, so no disclosing anything to your boyfriend, including the location."

A secret team-building drill seems suspicious. What does he have planned?

"Wait, what? I don't have a boyfriend."

I jerk my head up to look at him more closely. How did he get this impression?

"Who was the guy from last night? He definitely isn't a local or I would know him."

Having a male best friend shouldn't make people automatically think I'm unavailable. Not that it matters; I can't imagine Bear falling for someone like me.

"That's Toby, my best friend. We came here together."

He ponders over my words like he doesn't fully understand. "Don't tell him anything about the meeting. This information is for the enchanted forest only."

Hopefully tonight can help me become a certified member of this team. Although, I don't understand why there is a need for secrecy.

"Is this when I find out you're really a predator leading me astray?"

The words slip out before I've realised what I've said.

"Are you flirting with me?" he says with amusement.

My mouth drops open. Here I was thinking he could be some kind of serial killer, and he thinks I'm trying to flirt with him.

"Erm, no. How did you come up with that? It's not that you aren't attractive or anything." What on Earth am I saying? I bite my lip to stop myself from rambling further.

"Right. You're not one of those types of girls, are you?"

I'm so out of my depth. My cheeks begin to warm.

"I don't have a clue what you're talking about, but I have no intention of pursuing anything with you. I just want to keep my job."

I let out the breath I'd held in. My words were a little harsh, but he's running hot and cold. I'm finding it hard to keep up with him. It's like he's trying to give me whiplash.

"I'm just messing with you. You're cute when you're flustered."

Now my whole face is heating up. I can't get a read on this guy, which is confusing and frustrating. Tonight could be a way of getting back at me for my mistakes, but if I don't turn up, I might lose my job. I'm sworn to secrecy so I can't even ask my best friend for advice.

———

Toby has been acting sketchy since he got back to the campsite. I'm beginning to think he has a date with Sophie he doesn't want me to know about. Sitting on my tiny, creaky bed, I watch him pretend he isn't getting ready to go out. After showering, choosing a smart polo shirt, and dabbing himself with aftershave, he announces he's going for a walk. He doesn't give me a chance to answer before he's out the door. Usually I'd be annoyed by this dismissive behaviour, but tonight, it works in my favour.

Quickly, I wash my face, scoop my hair into a messy bun, and brush my teeth. Once dressed in my leggings and an oversized t-shirt, I slowly make my way to meet Bear. When I arrive, there's a group of about twenty familiar faces from around our zone in the park. They're discussing strategy while staring at a map of the area. Bear watches me approach. Vinnie puts his arm around me to pull me closer to the map as Bear draws two red crosses with a marker pen.

"You need to work on your time-keeping skills. I'm glad you could join us, Kara. Now, is everyone happy with the plan?"

I arrived with at least a minute to spare. Instead of pointing this out, I nod, acknowledging his comment.

The group respond to Bear with a mumble of yeses. I stare at his lips as he sets everyone up with their tasks. When the crowd disperses, he meets my eyes as my tongue darts out to wet my suddenly dry lips.

"Let's go."

"Wait. I don't know what we're doing."

"Capture the flag. Vinnie has the perfect location for ours. We need to get to the dark woods and find their flag. Come on."

Bear breaks into a run. It takes me a second to catch up with the game both mentally and physically.

Toby didn't have a date; he's on the other team. I've played this game before with some friends, so the rules are straightforward. Bear leads me into the forest area as we search for the opposition's flag. He takes the game deadly serious, making sure the coast is clear before moving out into the open. We stay close to the trees and out of sight as much as possible. I catch sight of Toby with a beautiful red-headed girl. Bear and I freeze our position, watching them move closer to our location. Bear signals for me to stay put as he tries to lead them away. The red-headed girl chases after him, but I lose sight of Toby.

As they move farther away, all I can hear are the noises of the forest. Every sound is crisp as I listen for some sign of Bear. A branch snaps, startling me. I turn to face the approaching footsteps when Toby appears in front of me. Sidestepping, I try to camouflage myself, but it's too late.

"Well, well, well... look who's keeping secrets," he says as he comes to stand next to me.

"I'm not the one who went for a 'stroll'." I cross my arms.

"Sleeping with the enemy, Toby?" An older, taller man appears behind him.

"Kara, this is Antony. He manages the dark woods zone."

I wave. "So, you're the guy I need to impress if I want to work in the haunted house?"

A deep laugh rumbles from his chest. "I like you.

Let me see what I can do, but for now, we should be on our way, newbie."

They both race off. Toby shouts, "See you at home," as they disappear out of sight. When I turn back around, I come face to face with Bear. Gasping, I pull my hand to my chest.

"You scared me."

"So, that's how it's going to be? I leave you for one second and you're already betraying us. Did you tell them where to find the flag while you were laughing at our team's expense?"

"It wasn't like that."

He holds his hand up to silence me. The scowl on his face returns, deepening its intensity. Guilt fills my stomach. Not because I gave the opposite team any answers, but because I want to swap my co-workers. The funny thing is, I'm not sure Bear's mood would improve if he understood the truth. Would he be happy to get rid of me? I can't please everyone, so I'm going to stop trying. I want to be in the dark woods, and there's nothing Bear, or anyone else, can say to stop me achieving my goal.

CHAPTER SEVENTEEN

KARA

There's a frosty feeling in the air for the next few days as Bear continues to ignore me. Finding someone to swap a zombie costume for a beautiful view is going to be tricky. Throwing my name badge into my locker, I let out a huff.

"It can't be that bad, honey."

Like magic, Lynne appears at my side. Untucking my shirt, I lift it over my head, leaving it in a heap.

"My boss hates me. It can't get any worse than that."

"I think you're being hard on yourself. He needs to warm up to you, that's all."

"If he could banish me, I'd be gone already. I've blown my chance to fit into the enchanted forest. The most I can hope for is an opening somewhere else."

"If Bear wanted you gone it would've already been done."

"What do you mean?"

"You still haven't figured out who he is?" she says with amusement.

I look at her blankly.

"Julian is the only son of Mr. Oaks, the park owner. Hasn't anyone told you? He's a kind soul, once you get to know him. I can't imagine him having bad feelings towards you, or anyone else, for that matter."

He really could fire me if he wanted. He's also so much more than I realised.

"Wait, rewind. Why do people call him Bear?"

"That's not my story to tell. But if he didn't like you, he would've got rid of you right from the start. His father will do anything to keep him happy."

"So, he could've traded me into the haunted house?"

She nods.

His dad owns the entire park. Julian, Bear, whatever his name is, could've moved me somewhere else in an instant. Why did he choose to keep me on his team when he doesn't like me? It doesn't make sense.

Once I've changed out of my work clothes, I set off to the campsite. The route has become familiar; between the trees and over the back gate. Toby is late, as usual, and the pod is in darkness. Instead of calling my sister, I use my phone to discover the real Julian. He really is an inspirational talent. It says he supports charities and is considered one of England's up and coming young people. I want to hate him for being so flawless, but I can't. Other than his mood swings towards me, he's practically perfect. The world is at his feet. I would kill to have his opportunities. By the end of the search, I have more questions than answers. Why didn't he want me to know who he is?

A shadow creeps over me as Toby tries to make me jump.

"You're too predictable," I say without turning to face him. I lock my phone and throw it onto the bed.

"I'm meeting Sophie at the pub if you're interested in joining us."

"I don't want to be a tag-along."

"You won't be. Besides, we're just friends. It will be good for you to finally meet her."

I'm not in the mood to socialise, but staying home alone will only prolong my negative mood.

"Sure. You're right. I'd like to get to know her."

———

All eyes turn to us as we enter the Frog and Goat. Tucking my hair behind my ear, my gaze meets Bear's. He doesn't bother to look away. Instead, he continues to watch me walk across the room, keeping his expression neutral.

The redhead from the night before is sitting at the table, which is already becoming our regular spot. Her long eyelashes flutter at Toby when she sees us. The smile on her face is warm and friendly as her attention sways to me.

"My two favourite women are in one place. I'll go get a round in while you two talk about me," Toby says.

Rolling my eyes, I take a seat next to Sophie. She waits for him to leave before she speaks.

"Give me some juicy gossip I can use against him tomorrow when he's trying to steal my hideout in the haunted house."

Laughing, I shake my head. "I think you're already keeping him on his toes."

"I'm jealous you've got such a great best friend. Mine has left me to travel around New Zealand for the summer. She'd saved every last penny to afford the trip and I can't begrudge her the experience of a lifetime."

"Why didn't you go with her?"

"What, and give up all this?" She uses her arms to gesture to her surroundings. "Besides, I'm going to start my epic adventure as soon as I finish university. Toby says you will be attending the same one too. Lancaster University is a good choice."

I smile. It'll be nice to have another familiar face around.

Toby returns with three pints of lager. Sophie raises her eyebrow, showing she approves of his choice. Taking a sip of my beer, my eyes wander over to Bear. He's talking to his friends with a smile on his face. He must save his scowls and brooding eyes for me.

"Don't tell me you've got a crush on Mr. Oaks himself. Take a number. Half the girls here wish he would look their way."

"I've got more chance of him throwing me off a cliff than him having romantic feelings towards me."

"Mike told me what happened." She points to the tall guy when she says Mike's name. "It's the funniest first day story this side of summer. I wouldn't waste your time on him, though. He doesn't date. Bear is too busy trying to save the world with his skateboard."

"If I could just get him to be my friend I'd be happy."

After talking to Sophie about her adventures, it's my turn to get the drinks in. I smile sweetly at the bartender when he catches my eye. He signals he won't be long as he carries a box of wine over to the fridge. Goosebumps prickle against my skin, sending an electrical pulse up my arm. I sense Bear before seeing him standing next to me. He's so close I can see the speckle of orange enhancing his eyes.

"I hope Sophie hasn't been saying too many bad things about me," he says.

"Why would she?" I ask, confused.

"Her crazy best friend wouldn't leave me alone last summer."

"Sophie seems nice. You shouldn't judge people by the actions of others."

Or for stupid mistakes, I silently add.

"I'm sure Sophie is lovely, but she isn't my number one fan. She might be different from her friend, but it doesn't mean she's not loyal to her."

I'm not sure if we're only talking about Sophie or if Bear is thinking about my loyalty to Toby. Making him question my trust wasn't my intention.

"I didn't tell the other team anything the other night. I'm sorry I gave you the impression I did. Can we start over? Hi. I'm Kara. I'm an occasional klutz, chocolate is my nemesis, and I would like to be friends with my boss."

I hold my hand out for him to shake, but instead, his lip twitches in amusement. "I'm sorry for overreacting. I'm not used to people surprising me."

I smile. Mending the bridge feels good. Let's hope I don't mess it up again.

"I'm full of surprises. All you've got to do is watch this space."

I flatten out my palms and join my thumbs together framing the space in front of me.

"If you're aiming for employee of the month, I'd give up now." His lip twitches as he tries to hide his smirk.

"After seeing inside Lynne's locker, I know I'm not equipped for that title. Although, I'd happily nominate her. Those red shoes were a lifesaver."

He smiles. "Here I was thinking you'd found the yellow brick road and it was Lynne all along."

I laugh. "The park has one of those?"

He laughs. "Sorry, princess. We've got a prehistoric dinosaur land and underwater world, but no Dorothy. You'll have to add the wonderful Wizard of Oz to the suggestion box."

"Maybe I'll do just that."

I raise my nose in the air, trying to act serious. It wouldn't be a bad suggestion. The theme park already has a fairy-tale theme in some of its zones. It could handle some more magic.

His attention is pulled towards his friends. I turn to look but they suspiciously turn away. Bear rubs the back of his neck. "I should go back to my friends before they start coming over. Be good. I'll see you in the morning."

I watch him walk away before going to join Toby and Sophie.

CHAPTER EIGHTEEN

BEAR

Beating the brush against the rubber mat, I push the excess water back into the lake. The sun is bright without a cloud in the sky. Sweat beads on my forehead, which I wipe away with the back of my hand. I pour a bottle of cold water over my head to cool myself down.

Kara's golden brown hair shimmers in the sun. Her back is facing me as her gaze follows someone on the main path. I use the opportunity to admire her beautiful curves. She's petite with a dainty hourglass figure, which isn't my usual type, yet there's something appealing about her.

Vinnie joins me on the edge of the deck. We stare out into the water as swan number two heads back towards us. Steadying the boat, I help the family out of the ride. The boat moves along to the entrance point and Kara steadies it for a young couple to step in. Vinnie leans close so nobody else can hear him.

"Have you got the new girl to forgive you for your grouchiness?" he teases.

"I'm not that bad."

"Dude, you've been a nightmare since your dad made you come home. A lesser girl might cry at your sour face."

I scowl at him. Vinnie is the only one who calls me out when he thinks I'm in the wrong. It wasn't my intention to be difficult with Kara. "I'll be more cheerful just for you. I'll even throw in an ice cream if you can guess which swan will come back next."

"I'm going for number four. Kara, what do you think? Bear says the ice creams are on him if we can guess which boat will dock first," Vinnie shouts over the rope to her. She moves closer towards us.

"Number seven has been out there the longest so I'll go for them," Kara says.

"They're too busy snogging to remember how to paddle. You're both going to lose this game," I say.

Two boats circle around the lake, coming in close. We watch patiently as they pass straight on by. The swans may not be the most exciting ride, yet it's one of my favourites. My dad gave me control of this side of the park and the boats became my special project. I chose the theme when we needed to revamp the ride. I could've chosen pirate ships or squids when I bought the new boats, however, with a little research I found, traditional swans appeal to a wider audience.

"How are you enjoying the summer?" Vinnie asks Kara.

"It's all good so far." She smiles, although it doesn't reach her eyes.

"See, I told you your grumpiness was upsetting the new girl."

I glare at him as Kara's eyebrows shoot up. She shakes her head, as if taken aback by his comment.

"Ignore him. He likes to stir up trouble," I say.

Shouting from the lake draws our attention to boat number seven. It rocks from side to side like an egg trying to right itself. I curse under my breath, pleading it doesn't capsize. Racing to the control room, I press the button on the microphone.

"Sit back down, boat number seven. This is not a game."

Vinnie is quicker to the speed boat than me. The idiot guy dramatically flings his arms wildly in the air as he belly flops into the lake. Another curse leaves my lips before I climb into the boat with Vinnie. He pulls the cord and the engine roars to life. As we approach, the lifesaving ring finds its target as it bounces into the water. We drag the guy onto the boat, and he arches over to cough up water. The blonde-haired girl in the swan looks apologetic when I climb in next to her. Setting the pedals in motion, I row us back to shore.

"I'm sorry. I shouldn't have pushed him in," she says.

"What the hell did he do to deserve your wrath?" I ask.

"He has arranged a date with someone else after spending all day making out with me."

"What a tool."

"I won't argue with that."

Kara helps me out of the boat when we reach the dock. I ignore the people nearby who are clapping at our rescue effort. After the girl exits the ride, Vinnie takes the couple to the sick bay.

"Are you sure you're not a witch? That was one crazy way to get the boat back into the shore."

"Skateballs. I'm so sorry. It's like I have an evil hex on me when it comes to you."

A laugh escapes my lips. "What are skateballs?"

She laughs nervously. "Did I say that out loud? Forget I said that. My nieces' made up words are rubbing off on me."

Her cheeks turn pink with a warm glow. She looks cute when I make her nervous. An unstoppable smile spreads across my face. I catch her staring at my lips, and I can't help wetting them with my tongue. A summer romance is not in the cards for me so I push down my train of thought. I'm sure she's a great girl, but I need to keep my focus on the park.

The antics of the crazy couple set a strange vibe. The swans are never the most popular attraction, but this is an unusual quiet spell. When Vinnie returns, he's holding three ice cream cones.

"Those two were insane. She's forgiven him and he's now taking her out tomorrow night instead of the other girl. I'll never understand women. He's obviously a bad apple."

"That's seriously messed up," I say.

"Who said romance is dead?" Kara says.

We eat our ice creams, staring out onto the lake. It's a hot day and the treat goes down easily.

"It's almost five-thirty. What do you say to us having a swan race?" I say, rubbing my palms together.

"It's on," Vinnie says.

"First one around the lake and feet back on the dock wins."

"Easy."

I didn't expect Kara to join us, yet she's hot on our tails.

Pedalling as fast as I can around the duck island, it's looking promising for me. That is until Vinnie has other ideas. He cuts me up, knocking me off course. Kara whips past us both, making it back to the dock first. I end up in last place, following closely behind Vinnie. We lie on the dock, trying to catch our breath. The smile on my face is genuine. My guard slips just for a moment when I see Kara's smile light up; she's beautiful.

CHAPTER NINETEEN

KARA

I'm later than usual leaving the changing room. The quiet atmosphere around the park gives way to the sound of the wildlife. The smell of freshly cut grass reminds me of home. I check my emails from my family. Opening the latest message, I smile at the cute picture of the four of them. Helen doesn't give me any clues to her relationship status with Derrick, although they look cosy together. The girls are surprised to hear Bear's a part of my adventure and fire questions at me. I tell them a few of the good things that have happened. They're enjoying their summer, although they say they miss me and my heart aches to be with them again.

Small twigs crunch under my feet as I move from the main path into the small woodland. My concentration stays with my phone until a squirrel jumps from a nearby branch. Stopping to admire the small creature, I hear a second pair of footsteps echoing in the distance. My heart begins to race when I don't see anyone approaching. Studying the trees, nothing looks suspicious. I loop back around and hide behind a large trunk, waiting to see if anyone appears. My breath hitches as someone begins to move towards me. To steady my nerves, I count to ten, waiting for the person to move closer. I leap out from behind the tree and push the rock hard body against the bark. My eyes wander up his face, lingering on his lips before I meet Bear's brooding eyes. The surprise on his face would be comical if I didn't feel so on edge.

"What are you doing? You almost gave me a heart attack!"

My adrenaline is still working overtime.

"Whoa, you're strong for a little thing." He smiles with amusement.

I hold him tightly in place, although he could probably push me away if he wanted to. We stare at each other, neither one of us willing to back down.

"I'm not sure that was a compliment. Why are you following me?"

The stiffness in his shoulders loosens. His face is unreadable. "It's not safe for you to be walking around these woods alone."

I'm a modern day woman and capable of looking after myself. Besides, why would he care what happens to me? We haven't known each other that long and we're only co-workers. "Strange men like you could be following me, you mean?"

He frowns. "For all you know, there could be a serial killer lurking in these woods."

"Or a potential stalker?"

We stare at each other without speaking for a second. Why is he so confusing?

"Sorry for looking out for you." His words almost sound like an accusation. I haven't done anything wrong.

"It's the middle of summer and as light as midday. Besides, I'm a big girl. I can look after myself. What have I done to make you think otherwise?"

"I bet all murder victims say that."

He's trying to make me laugh. My eyes soften, although I keep my expression neutral.

"When was the last time anything remotely interesting happened here? The only thing that's scary is the theme park rides, and they are built for thrills."

His lips tighten. As we stare at each other, I slowly become aware of where we are. The surrounding forest begins to breathe again as the tension leaves my body. I ease away, allowing him to regain his balance.

"Why didn't you just ask if you could walk me home?"

"I didn't want you to get the wrong idea."

I roll my eyes. "Get over yourself."

"I'm handling this all wrong. I'm not your enemy. Let me walk you home. Please."

This boy confuses me more than anyone I've ever met. I don't think he'll take no for an answer. Instead of answering him, I set my feet in motion. He easily falls into step beside me.

"Have you followed me before?"

"Since the first day. The lake incident didn't fill me with confidence that you were streetwise. Plus, it's on my route home."

"If you hadn't been speeding down the path, neither of us would've fallen in."

"So now it's my fault?"

"No. That's not what I'm saying. You can walk me home, but stop making out that I'm some fragile princess."

I've been looking after myself since I was young; I'm independent and nobody has ever wrapped me in cotton wool. On the other hand, it's only a walk home and it's on his way anyway. I don't want to make a big deal over nothing, so I can accept this small gesture.

"Okay, I can do that."

I run my hand through my hair and an uncontrollable smile spreads across my face. When I look at Bear, he's smiling too. Having a male best friend should help me understand boys, but it doesn't. Once I reach the fence, we mumble our goodbyes and he watches me as I enter the pod area. For the first time, Toby has beaten me home. The door is wide open and his wet towel is blowing in the wind. When he sees me approaching, he races over and spins me around like when we were kids.

"What's got into you?" I smile as he puts me back down.

"You're late home and I have news I'm busting to tell you." His own smile sets in place.

"Have you got a date with Sophie?"

"No, although I seem to be making progress, she just needs a little more time. Josh is applying for a manager's job, and if he gets it, there will be an opening in the haunted house. You'll be able to join the scare team." He makes claws with his hands while groaning monster noises.

"That's great news." I try to sound happy.

Joining Toby on his summer adventure is what I wanted, so why do I feel like it could be a mistake? I'm beginning to like the team I'm working with. It might not be as exciting as the haunted house, however, today was fun. In his own way, Bear seems to be warming to me too.

After showering, Toby and I eat beans on toast for tea and play card games. A quiet night in is what I need, although it doesn't help shake my unsettled feeling.

CHAPTER TWENTY

KARA

Drinking from a paper cup, Bear waits for me on the far side of the fence. I tuck my hair behind my ear before jumping over into the woodland. He passes me my own drink which has *tea* written on the side.

"How did you know I'm a tea drinker?"

"I thought you understood my stance after yesterday's conversation. I'm your personal stalker, remember?"

"Vinnie told you."

He nods in acknowledgement.

"Next time I'll bring croissants if the hot drink is going to be part of our regular routine," I say.

"You drive a hard bargain, but it's a deal." We smile at each other.

"Alice from one of the caravans makes them every

morning. They're delicious." My stomach rumbles at the thought of her baking.

"I bet. Do you like sleeping in the pod?"

Sipping our drinks, we make our way onto the main path. People wave at Bear as we pass.

"The idea of sleeping in my own bed sounds like heaven, but it's not so bad."

"How does the whole boy, girl, and a tiny pod work?"

"Same way it would with anyone else. We have rules. I'm lucky Toby likes to be tidy. I've not really had my own space since my mum left. Keeping my belongings in a box doesn't bother me. Actually, it's kind of normal in my world."

"Where's your mum?"

"She went to pursue her dreams of being a singer on cruise ships soon after my sixteenth birthday. Once I was technically an adult, she said I didn't need her anymore and it was time for her to fulfil her own destiny. I don't speak to her anymore and my father is far from a good role model. My sister is the only family who looks after me. We have each other. Well, until I came here, that is. What about you?"

"It's just me and my dad. We get along most of the time. He has high expectations of me which sometimes overshadows his judgement, but I can handle him."

"At least he cares," I say with a little sadness in my voice. I wish my own dad cared about what I did.

He offers me a small smile hopefully missing my moment of gloominess.

I wave goodbye to Bear and make my way into the changing room. Pink ruffles fill the small area as Lynne squeezes herself into an outrageously sparkly outfit. I bang on my locker door and it opens on the third try. I change quickly, wondering if Bear will be waiting outside. I shake off the silly thought. The swans are so close, he has no reason not to wander across to them. I'm ready before Lynne, and I help fasten her dress.

"You look happier today. Did you make friends with Bear or is there a new reason to be cheerful?"

"It's looking better between us."

"Good for you. Thanks for helping me with the dress."

"You're welcome."

Lynne reapplies her bright fuchsia lipstick in the mirror. She offers it to me, though I decline. It's the type of colour that would turn heads and I'm hoping to keep a low profile rather than draw attention to myself.

"A group of us meet by the bandstand every lunchtime. You should come."

"Thanks. Maybe I will."

I've been using my breaks to sit by the river, reading fantasy romance novels. Having company is a good idea to help me get to know people, although I enjoy my quiet time. Exiting the changing room, I find Bear talking to one of the fairies.

"You didn't have to wait," I say once we're back en-route.

He shrugs like it's no big deal. "What are you planning to do with your days off?"

"Toby and I are going to check out the university campus in Lancaster. It's not too far from here and we start in September."

He breaks eye contact to look across the lake. The corners of his lips turn down for a split second before he recovers. Surely he can't be upset I'll be sticking around for more than the summer?

———

Lying on the small camp bed with my hands behind my head, I wait for Toby to come home. It's his turn to be late again. The smell of burning toast fills the air while a smoke alarm beeps in the background. I catch sight of Alice wafting a blue towel out of her caravan door. I get up to offer my help when a picture of Helen appears on my phone.

Multiple greetings from my family sing through the speaker when I accept the call. My smile is instant.

"I hope you're staying out of trouble," Helen says, teasing.

"Of course. Nothing exciting is happening here."

"You're just saying that to make us feel better. I miss you," Anna says.

"Aww, I miss you girls too."

"We saw Mum kissing Dad," Hayley squeals.

I can hear them laughing as they wrestle over the phone.

"Let's pretend Hayley didn't say that. Have you met anyone interesting?"

"I've made some new friends. I even have a fairy godmother."

I fill them in on Lynne's fairy-isms. I briefly mention Toby and Bear, trying not to linger on the details as I don't want to answer any questions about them. I'm starting to like it here in Blue Oaks, but I miss my family. Just as I end the call, I hear the creak of footsteps. Toby appears, already changed out of his scary costume. He turns the kettle on, waving a cup at me.

"Hey. How was your day?" I say.

"I've had another great day scaring unsuspecting parents."

He laughs while I shake my head. "You'll be sending someone to an early grave. At least they'll get a rest tomorrow. Speaking of which, there's a train at ten in the morning. We can be at the campus by half past."

"Yeah, about that. Can we take a rain check? We've plenty of time before the end of summer and I have a date with Sophie. She's finally giving me a chance," he says excitedly.

I'm happy for Toby, although I can't hide my disappointment. I want to be the one spending the day with him. He carries on making the tea and doesn't seem to notice my wavering smile.

"Where're you taking her?"

"There's an old style theatre on the edge of town. Sophie wants to go there. Apparently, it has its original seats and smells of buttery popcorn. It sounds brilliant. If you've nothing better to do, you can always come with us."

"No. I don't want to ruin your date. I'll be fine. There's plenty to do around here."

"We have tonight together. We can do anything you like. Paint our nails, or do our hair." He's trying to make me laugh. The faintest whisper of a smile threatens to appear on my face.

"Lynne might have your colour. We could borrow nail varnish from her."

"How about I treat us to a takeaway and we play some cards?"

"I could eat a Chinese."

He flicks me on the arm before wandering off to order the food. I lie on the bed, staring at the ceiling and thinking about what I'm going to do with my time tomorrow.

CHAPTER TWENTY ONE

BEAR

The board leaves the ramp as easily as a swan glides onto a pond. I twist in the air until me and the board swing back on to the half-pipe. A perfect McTwist, even if I say so myself. Removing my helmet, I make my way inside for a drink.

My dad is sitting at the table, working on his latest project; his reading glasses balance on the end of his nose. I fill a glass with water and drink it down in one smooth gulp.

"Julian, please take a look at this for a minute."

Peering over his shoulder, I look at the two designs. Both of the architectural drawings he's looking at are unique in their own way. I've looked at ride and feature plans before. I like both designs.

"What do you think? The jungle design is colourful, although the ocean has an octopus fountain." He runs his fingers over the page before lifting his eyes to me.

I look at the plans closely. I want to give a concise answer to show I can. Either option would be fine, but I saw an article on a new aquarium which proved to be popular. The sea design has potential for some colourful fish and maybe something for younger visitors. "The ocean one is my favourite."

"Thanks. It's mine too."

He goes back to staring at the drawings while scribbling numbers on his notepad. I watch him for a few seconds longer before heading out the door. I'm covering lunch for Vinnie as we're short on staff today. As soon as my feet touch my board, I'm gliding along the main slope to the park. Vinnie offers a fist bump when I reach the deck. For the next hour, I work with Chloe to help keep the ride running smoothly. Time passes quickly. When I step off the deck, the beautiful brunette I'm spending way too much time thinking about is awkwardly trying to carry a dusky pink bag, the contents of which is flapping all over the place. Amusement plays on my lips until the load starts to tumble out. The smile on my face broadens as I quickly hurry over to help her.

"I thought you were going out of town? If you were trying to avoid me, you should've found a better hiding place."

Her curls fall in front of her face, hiding her pretty blue eyes. I lean down to help pick up her laundry.

"Toby has a date which leaves me to my own devices for the day."

"Maybe I should apply for the position of your best friend. I'd make a better sidekick."

"What qualities do you have?"

I laugh. Taking the bag, I balance it on my skateboard, pulling it close to my chest.

"I have a laundry room, if that helps. Using the washing machine might be something I can handle."

Someone else washes my clothes, but Kara makes me want to do this small favour for her. Whenever I make her smile, it gives me a warm feeling inside, and I can't keep my distance. Besides, being her friend can't hurt, right? It's not like I'm spending all my free time with her, and I was free today anyway.

"You don't have a housekeeper?"

"I didn't say that, but for you, I'll get my hands dirty."

"With an offer like that, how can a girl refuse?"

That warm feeling returns when she smiles at me. It's just a friendly gesture; it doesn't mean anything. There is no need for me to overthink it.

"Come on. I'll give you the behind-the-scenes tour."

"*Now* I feel special."

"I wouldn't carry a pink pillowcase for just anyone." I wink at her and she smiles in response.

"It's the biggest bag I could carry. I forgot to take my uniform home last night."

The closer we get to my house, the wider her eyes become. I don't bring many people here. My ex-girlfriend took great pleasure in telling people about where I live and it made me uncomfortable. Our relationship only lasted three months and I haven't dated since. Her enthusiasm for my possessions felt stronger than her feelings for me. It put me off girls and I don't want to feel used again. I haven't dated for over a year, but I sense Kara is different. I pinch my arm to remind myself we are just friends.

"You actually live here?"

Blue Oaks mansion stands tall in its eighteen-century glory. I can appreciate the beauty of the building with its long, narrow windows and over the top décor. Although to me, this is just home.

"Don't be getting any gold digger ideas," I joke.

"Don't worry, I won't get any romantic feelings towards you. I don't want your head getting any bigger."

The thought of her writing me off makes me frown, even though I probably deserve it after what I said. Her words shouldn't have an effect on me. I'm not looking for a friend with benefits or a girlfriend, but that doesn't stop the disappointment settling in my chest.

"You're a funny girl."

"I try."

"Don't forget to remove your shoes and put on carpet protectors," I say as we walk through the door.

Her eyes go wide as she looks around. I burst out laughing.

"It was a joke. I can be funny too."

She jabs me in the arm.

We make our way down to the basement. I put her laundry into the washing machine, and sprinkle some powder into the pot. A spark of mischief still lingers in my mind. Reaching into the ironing pile, I pull out a clean pair of socks which I launch at Kara. They fly straight over her shoulder, softly grazing the side of her neck. She looks at me with shocked, wide eyes. Indecision flickers across her face before she grabs a handful of socks, throwing them at me. Laundry begins to dart in all directions. Her laughter echoes around the room, making my own chase after it. My smile mirrors hers. We hold eye contact for a few seconds before I look away.

"I have an idea. Do you trust me?" I ask, ready to share some of my private life with her.

She touches her lip with her finger, playfully thinking over my question. Being close to Kara is easy. It's like she fits, even if I'm trying to fight my feelings. Once she gives her approval, I lead her to the skate park in the grounds of my house.

I watch her take in my world; the cement half-pipe, ramps, and grind rail have been here for years. My dad had them made for my eighth birthday. Kara doesn't seem as overwhelmed as she did with the size of my house which is great. I lead her to the equip-ment shed and she peers in.

"Everything is black. I hope you can cope without a touch of sparkle. I don't have any fancy trimmings like Lynne," I tease.

"Simple is better sometimes. Wait, you don't want me to get on that death trap, do you?" She looks at the skateboard.

"You'll be fine. Besides, you entertained the idea before we left Northumberland."

She rubs her arm. She's nervous, although she doesn't voice it.

Kara places the helmet on her head, squashing her thick brown hair down. Stepping onto the board, she holds her hands out to me. Slowly, I pull her forward. Her smile drops for a second as cute worry lines appear on her forehead under the helmet. Her big blue eyes meet mine and her smile returns with confi-dence. I show her a couple of simple moves which she quickly picks up.

"I've got to ask, why does everybody call you Bear?"

"So, the bear is out of the bag. You know that's not my real name. I guess my secret is out."

She looks down at her feet. "It's okay. You don't have to tell me if you don't want to."

"No it's fine. I sort of stumbled into it and the name stuck. I'm like the Milky Bar Kid of Blue Oaks."

She meets my gaze and her nose wrinkles. "You

sell chocolate?"

A laugh escapes my lips. I wish that was all there was to it. "I did some promotional shoots for the park when I was younger."

"You were a cute bear?" she asks, biting her lip to hold back a smile.

"When you do that one thing that ends up being bigger than life, it's hard to shake. Instead of hiding from the name, I embrace it. When I became part of the urban circuit, the nickname fit easily so I just rolled with it."

"So, you're a famous bear. Don't think for a second I'm not going to check the pictures out."

A laugh rumbles through my chest. Wait. She said 'cute bear'. Most people want a giggle when they search for my pictures.

"What about you? What's your superpower?"

"I don't have one."

"There must be something you're good at."

"Sorry. I'm completely talentless, unless you consider alienating people and making them want to throw darts at my picture."

"That was only one time," I joke. "You're not that bad."

"The famous Julian Oaks actually gave me a compliment."

Making her smile does something to me that I can't explain. Kara is a sweet girl and I want to know more about her. Oh, boy. I'm in trouble.

CHAPTER TWENTY TWO

KARA

"You were home late last night," I say to Toby as he emerges from the pod. He stretches his arms above his head, letting out a groan. Slumping into the deck chair beside me, he rubs his hand over his face.

"We went to the pub. I think I'm coming down with something. My head's throbbing like I've been hit with a baseball bat."

"You mean you're hungover. I have no sympathy for you at all. Knowing your limit is half the battle."

"Sophie is wild. The drinks were flowing like water. Plus, that girl can handle her drink. I couldn't keep up with her. Last night was the best first date I ever had, and I'm including the date with Olivia Henson from year six."

I roll my eyes. "Olivia Henson was not your date. Her mum gave you a lift home one time."

"It did count."

"I'm glad you had a good time. Sophie is nice.

"I hope you didn't miss me too much."

I shrug, not wanting to express my opinion. I had a great day. Surely he didn't think I was going to sit around waiting for him to return all day.

Toby frowns and I follow his gaze. Bear is walking towards us, looking fresh and clean cut. Nothing like Toby and me, who look like the token rough campers. My forgotten washing is neatly packed in a clear, airtight pouch. Toby raises an eyebrow at me with a curious expression on his face.

"I'll go get some breakfast from Alice. I'm sure she can muster something up for her favourite customer," Toby says, rubbing his hands together.

Bear places my washing on the decking, leaning against the side rail.

"So, this is how the other half lives," he says with a kind smile.

"Welcome to my mansion. I'd give you a tour, but what you can see is what you get."

"You really are living it up. I would be jealous if I didn't have a king-size bed made of the fluffiest materials known to man."

"I could swap you if you insist. Although, I don't think a rich boy like you could handle all of this." I raise my arms in the air, gesturing to the pod. He laughs softly.

Toby returns with three croissants which he hands

out before slumping back into his chair. Bear sits on the stairs, showing no sign of leaving. I shouldn't be so happy he's come to see me, but I am.

"You get a full day to do anything you want and the best thing you could come up with is laundry?" Toby says.

"Actually, I went skateboarding."

Toby almost chokes on his croissant, laughing. "Now that I would like to see." He checks me over. "I can't see any injuries. There are no signs of bruising or cuts. It looks like you survived this time." I swat him off as he tries to turn my arm over.

"So, I'm not a bad luck charm?" Bear says, taking my attention away from Toby. My smile returns as we fall into our teasing ways.

"I made one mistake. One time. It's not like I'm a walking disaster," I laugh.

"I still wouldn't have put you on a skateboard," Toby sniggers.

Toby is acting overprotective. It's not like I've never tried anything new before. If I said I wanted to go skating with him, he wouldn't have second guessed it. Toby finishes his last mouthful of food, grabs a towel, and excuses himself for a shower. Out of Bear's sight, Toby gives me a questioning look and I give a sharp nod to tell him everything is fine.

"Has Toby got plans with Sophie again today?" Bear asks.

"I don't know, to be honest."

"Do you think he would mind if I stole you? I'm warning you, it won't be all fun and games. I have an important task I could use a hand with."

"Okay, I'm curious. Your plan sounds intriguing. Toby left me yesterday, so I don't see me disappearing on him today as a problem."

Before I know it, I'm following Bear out of the campsite and into a car.

Forty-five minutes later, I'm wearing dark overalls, painting white walls in a local nursing home. The paint flicks back into my hair as the roller glides up the wall. There are five small teams decorating different areas of the nursing home. Bear and I are in the dining hall.

"Frank the groundskeeper is always desperate for volunteers. I try to help whenever possible."

"You're too close to perfect." My words trail off when I release what I'm confessing.

My cheeks turn pink at the compliment I didn't mean to give. From what I've seen so far, he's charitable, kind, and always thinking of others. I could never match his qualities. His future girlfriend is one lucky girl.

"I hope you don't mind doing this. Sorry it's not more exciting."

Another layer of paint splatters into my hair as I work the roller up the next patch of wall. Helping with this project is fun and I'm enjoying the company. I may not be great at the job, but I'm doing my best.

"I have no complaints."

"There's something about you, Kara," he whispers, his voice gravelly.

His gaze is intense. He blinks a few times before coming back to the present. It's Bear's turn to blush, which makes me smile. His eyes never leave mine as his thumb brushes paint from my chin.

"I'm going to need a shower after this," I say.

"I agree with you there. I, on the other hand, don't have a speck of paint on me."

"We can soon change that." I laugh.

He darts away from me and I chase him with the roller. Paint smears across his arms when I catch up to him.

"You didn't just do that."

Frozen to the spot, I wait for his reaction, unsure what he'll do. He takes the opportunity to wipe some paint from his forearm onto my face. He chases me back across the room until I have nowhere to go. My back is up against the cold drywall. Bear stands tall in front of me. His strong arms rest on each side of my head. His laughter softens as he looks into my eyes. He brings his palm to my face and slowly smears paint over my cheek then raises his eyebrow in amusement as he steps away, laughing.

"If you paint slower, you'll get more of it on the wall."

He shows me his technique. We glance at each

other every so often in between paint refills, but neither of us speaks.

It takes us most of the day, but the finished result is worth it. Seeing the smile on Frank's face makes me feel good about myself. I can see why Bear likes to help, and if he asks me to assist him again I'd happily say yes. I've enjoyed spending time without my family and Toby.

————

Toby is lying on his bed when I walk into the camping pod. The lights are on and the door is wide open. Music plays softly in the background.

"Where've you been and why do you look different?" he asks.

A strange smirk flickers across his face. Is he thinking my day with Bear was full of corruption rather than the innocent truth? I give the details of my task, making sure to include the fact I got a hot shower in a decent bathroom.

"Did you spend some of your time with Sophie or have you been in bed since I left?"

"No, I didn't sleep all day. I hung around here feeling sorry for myself. Ditching you yesterday was a mistake. The next free day we have together we're going to take that trip to the university, I promise."

His face is full of remorse which is usual for him. I shouldn't be happy he missed me, but I am. It would be nice if he thought of me first for once instead of his own needs. Something is on his mind. I can see it processing behind his eyes, but he doesn't share his thoughts and I don't push for answers. He'll tell me when he's ready.

After a few rounds of Rummy with the cards, I fall asleep listening to one of Toby's playlists. Bear stroking my cheek plays in my sweet dreams.

CHAPTER TWENTY THREE

KARA

"Here comes trouble," Vinnie says as I return from my lunch break by the lake.

My tranquil spot has become a secret. It's the same place I've sat for lunch since the first day, but somehow, it's become my hidden sanctuary. One I'm not willing to share with the curious boys. Casually, I walk onto the deck and put my lifejacket back on.

"You've got ice cream on your face," Bear says with amusement.

I rub my cheek, even though I know he's lying. A tuna sandwich and an apple made up my lunch. There wasn't a dessert in sight.

Vinnie shields his eyes, searching the people passing by.

"Didn't your mystery man walk you back after your secret rendezvous?" Vinnie asks.

"You're not going to trip me up, Vinnie. My hour of freedom is all mine. You don't have to worry about what I get up to."

"Don't tell me you're like Bear and waiting for your soulmate to show up with a neon sign before you'll start dating?"

Bear's scowl brightens my smile. I find Vinnie's statement as amusing as he does.

"I'm waiting for the right girl, not a marriage proposal. The 29th of February won't be a special day for me." He shakes his head, looking unimpressed with Vinnie.

"You'll be waiting a long time for an Irish legend that only happens on a leap year," I say with a laugh.

"The closest Bear has gotten to a girl in over a year is you, Kara. That's only because you're on our team."

"My priority is to get on the same page as my dad. I don't have time for distractions."

"Bear here is a modern day Robin Hood. He spends his free time saving the world."

Bear rolls his eyes at Vinnie's words, confirming the suspicion I already have. He's one of the good guys.

"Just because I'm not trying to pick up girls in the pub, doesn't mean I'm some kind of saint."

A rhythmic knocking sound on the deck brings us out of our conversation. An older guy in a smart-looking suit walks slowly towards us. When he draws closer, I instantly recognise his distinct features. It's

Mr Oaks, although Bear doesn't hurry to meet him. Instead, he stands up taller and his posture tenses. Once he reaches us, we wait for him to speak.

"I need a word."

Bear's face tightens at his dad's words. Vinnie pulls me closer to the edge of the lake as a family arrives back at the dock.

"We'd best leave them to it," Vinnie voice is tight leaving no room for me to question him.

"I know where Bear gets his brooding looks from now," I say, trying to lighten the mood.

"It can't be good news if his dad's come all the way down here. Hopefully Bear won't be too grumpy after he leaves."

My smile fades. Bear has given me glimpses into his life, but I'm on the outside. Thinking back to the conversation about the mad king, I try to fit the disjointed pieces together. Vinnie settles a young couple into a swan, warning them to stay inside the boat. I bite my lip to stop a laugh escaping.

"What did he want?" Vinnie asks when Bear returns, though his face remains unreadable.

"He has to go out of town for a few days."

"It's settled then. Party time at the mansion," Vinnie says with a hopeful look.

"More like he wants me to attend a charity dinner he committed to months ago."

"If you're asking me on a date, I could be free for you tonight," Vinnie jokes.

"I already know how that evening plays out. It ends with me alone while you chat up some poor waitress and drink too much beer at the open bar. I think I'll pass."

"Hey, give me some credit. Sophistication is my middle name. I'll drink gin and tonic with a chase of olives."

"Actually, I'm hoping Kara will go with me." His words come out evenly, like this is no big deal.

I blink in disbelief while my brain catches up with what he's said. He wants me to be his date? Is this like when I've helped Toby out, or does this mean something more? Bear said he didn't have time for distractions. He must just need a friendly face. One who won't prop up the bar and ignore him.

"I'm not sure you can handle a night with me," I tease.

"You can wear flat shoes. You don't have to make much effort and we won't stay out late. We only need to be there for an hour or two."

At least Toby would try and make me feel special. Bear is asking me like he's bored thinking about going which is charming to say he wants my company. He could have tried to sell it to me with a proper hot meal. I'm an easy girl to please, but his proposal is lame even by my standards.

"You make it sound so dreamy," I say, and Vinnie laughs.

Bear shakes his head. "I meant I'll agree to any of

your terms. You can have the afternoon off to find a dress if it will make you happy."

Scratch that. Bear and Toby are not alike at all. The night is sounding like a chore.

"You're so romantic. How can a girl say no?"

He closes his eyes for a second. He huffs out a breath as he opens them. "Okay, I'll try a different approach. I don't want to go on my own. Please will you come with me?"

I can hear the desperation in his voice and it makes me want to laugh, even if it would be mean. Let's hope he's more charming to girls he *wants* to take out.

"You're hopeless. Assuming it isn't a real date, I'll accept, but I don't want to go shopping. I'm not that type of girl. Can't you use your crystal ball to find me something to wear?"

"I'll use my resources and have something sent to your pod."

He pulls out his phone and signals he's going to make some calls. Vinnie laughs like he knows a secret and nudges my foot. I give him a little push before going to help a couple get out of a boat. I'm not sure what he thinks he knows, but I'm not entertaining his idea.

————

After work, Bear walks me to the fence, giving me no hint of what is waiting for me at the pod. Once I'm alone, my curiosity quickens my step. Bear wasn't interested in going tonight, so what could he have found me to wear? I hope he put a bit of effort into finding me an outfit. Although, he probably doesn't care what I look like. All I can hope for is something not too short and in my size.

Lynne is waiting for me on the deck. I instantly feel more confident. Her outfits are always gorgeous, and I don't mean her costumes. She pulls me into a hug. The twinkle in her eyes tells me she's excited. Make-up and dressing up have never been my thing but it will be nice to have this moment with Lynne. Toby appears from the pod and gives Lynne a cup of tea while she points to my towel. My life just became a teen movie; one where I'm the star, and I'm not used to being the centre of attention.

After I shower, she dries my hair and puts make-up on my face. Lynne seems to enjoy making me up, and it isn't the worst experience I've ever had. She holds false lashes up and I shake my head.

"The eyelashes are too much."

I know they're fashionable but that's where I'm drawing the line. The make-up already feels heavier than what I'd usually wear. I don't need to overdo it, especially when this isn't a date.

"Okay. No false eyelashes. Let's take a look at the dresses."

She opens her theatre-style costume box and shows me three completely different outfits. Holding each one up against herself, she dances around. They range from a pink cocktail dress, to a short green number. I'm not the type of girl who gets excitement from clothes, but I'm enjoying watching Lynne in her element.

"You can choose," I say nervously.

Her lips turn up into a genuine smile. She passes me a figure-hugging off the shoulder yellow dress. It has ruffles and gold sequin detail. I think about arguing for a split second, except I trust her judgement. All these dresses are out of my comfort zone. At least the shoes she picks are flat sparkly sandals.

"Stop fidgeting, you look stunning," she scolds once I'm ready. Toby's mouth hangs open when he catches sight of me.

"Next time you step in as my date, I'm going to hire Lynne to dress you up. You look beautiful," Toby says.

His comment sounds harsh, but I'm guessing that wasn't his intention. I may not wear a lot of make-up, but I *do* make an effort when we go out. Rolling my eyes, I head for the mirror. The person before me is nothing like my usual casual self. I feel like a prom queen on her special night.

CHAPTER TWENTY FOUR

KARA

Taking Bear's arm, he leads me into the banquet hall. The magnificent décor doesn't help my nerves as I pull the hem of my dress down for the fifth time since we arrived. Shiny helium balloons are spread through the room, giving the place a golden glow. All the men wear black and white, without a splash of colour. Each lady holds her head high with sophistication. Their dresses are classy, stylish, and compliment their figures. I feel out of place, like I should be helping serve the food, not eating it.

Bear works the room. He shakes a few people's hands on his way to our table, although he only offers minimal conversation. He pulls out my chair which has a red velvet cover and I take a seat. My gaze wanders around the room, taking in the expensive silverware and lavish champagne bottles. When my attention returns to the present, Bear's eyes are on me. I'm about to tell him how awkward I feel when his words distract me.

"You look really pretty tonight."

"Thanks. I'll take the compliment, even though I know you've got to say it." I nervously tuck a strand of hair behind my ear. His eyes follow my hand as it brushes along my skin. I wish I knew what he was thinking, but I'm not bold enough to ask.

He leans in close and I meet him halfway. The words he whispers tingle across my skin. "You'd think these people lead boring lives, but it's far from the truth. See the lady on table five in the black sequin dress?"

"The graceful older lady?"

"Yes. She's in her eighties and runs a burlesque class."

My eyes widen in surprise. She doesn't look a day over sixty. Her nose is high in the air and there isn't a trace of a smile. Her jewellery looks more expensive than my entire life's possessions.

"And the lady over there by the bar in the green dress writes raunchy adult novels. Every single person here has a colourful story to tell."

"What about you? Tell me your deepest darkest secrets," I tease.

"Wouldn't you like to know." His tone is light and playful.

We smile at each other.

"Why don't you want to come to these events? These people seem interesting. I thought you liked helping charities."

"Everything about these nights is completely fake. Hardly any of the people here care about the good cause. It's a pointless exercise to help them feel better about themselves. The money would be better spent directly with the charities, or if they donated their time, which they'll never do because it's beneath them."

"Why is this important to your dad?"

"For my old man, it's all about business. These people are his connections. Being in the know at the right time can be a game-changer when it comes to a successful deal."

The ring of someone tapping a spoon on a glass silences the room.

"Ladies and gentlemen, please take your seats. Dinner will be served shortly," a loud voice announces.

The waitresses hands out glasses of bubbly in champagne flutes. A woman in a maroon dress with bright red lipstick sits next to me. She smiles when she sees Bear sitting beside me.

"Evening, Julian. This must be your girlfriend. She's very pretty. You're a lucky guy."

We speak at the same time.

He says, "Thank you."

And I say, "Julian and I are just friends."

Her smile deepens at our conflict.

"Beatrice, this is my good friend Kara."

"Lovely to meet you Kara." She offers a warm smile. "Where's your father?" she asks, looking around.

"Unfortunately, he had to go out of town."

She looks disappointed. "That's such a shame. I was hoping to speak with him."

"His plans for the new zone are already taking shape and I think you'll find them inspiring."

"You're a tease. Graham won't show me the designs until he's finished. I'll admit I'm intrigued."

"I promise it will be worth the wait. Let's say greens, blues, and purples are going to be a big hit."

"Come on, Julian. You can give me more than that." She pouts. Beatrice is making me curious about what happens behind the scenes at the theme park.

He laughs. "My dad won't mind me giving you a little more information supposing he is hoping to get you on board." He exaggerates the last word.

"Should I be looking over the starboard?"

"Way over. Try closer to the anchor."

She gives a knowing look. "My lips are sealed. Thank you."

A couple take their seats at our table and Beatrice turns to greet them. Julian leans in close to me again.

"Beatrice makes the fairy costumes. Lynne's outfits are her masterpieces. Unfortunately, she also has a hopeless crush on my dad. I understand now why he didn't want to come tonight. He must be going through one of his avoiding her stages. A request to sit next to him will have had him in a tailspin. My dad doesn't want to tell her he's not interested. I should've seen the signs. He's been acting strangely since the last time they met up."

"She seems lovely."

"She is. My dad isn't interested in dating anyone though. He hasn't been on one single date since my mum died."

"I'm sorry. I didn't know."

"It was a long time ago." His words are dismissive, and I'm guessing he doesn't want to talk about it.

The knife easily cuts through the succulent chicken. My usual beans on toast do not compare to the fresh vegetables. I savour every mouthful. Beatrice smiles when she catches my eye.

"Julian tells me you're a costume designer. My sister works in a sewing mill. She wishes she could design her own accessories, but so far, I'm the only one who owns her prototypes," I say to Beatrice as I sip my champagne.

"You'll have to show me some of her designs. I'm always on the lookout for new talent."

"Sure. I have a few things with me at the camping pod."

"You're staying at the campsite?"

"Yes. I'm here for the summer before I go to university."

"Is Julian treating you well?"

"He's not so bad as a boss," I say with a playful smirk on my face. Julian responds with a fake scowl which broadens my smile.

"She's cute, Julian." She laughs.

"Lynne's outfits are stunning. They match her personality flawlessly." I genuinely believe my words.

"Thank you." She unclasps her purse and hands me her card. "Tell your sister to contact me to discuss her work. It's lovely to meet you. Please excuse me. I need to powder my nose."

She stands and makes her way across the room.

"Remind me not to let you get too close to my dad," Bear says.

"What do you mean?" I ask.

"Your networking skills would make him proud. Who knows what task he'd rope you in to doing next."

"Do you think I should pass on her details to my sister?" I ask nervously. I don't want to get Helen's hopes up if Beatrice was just being polite.

"Absolutely. She works miracles for small businesses."

After the food, Julian moves us onto the dance floor. Even with my resistance to dance, he doesn't take no for an answer. He pulls me in tight while I try not to step on his feet. I don't know any fancy dances, but Julian seems content with a simple sway.

"Thank you for coming with me tonight. I'm having a nice time."

"Me too. This is a first for me; I don't usually attend fancy meals. Being a stand-in date for Toby when he's upset his latest conquest is about as exciting as my life gets."

"Didn't any of your boyfriends take you out?"

"I haven't had a serious relationship. I went to prom with Toby."

"He's a lucky guy." There's an edge to his voice I don't understand.

He hugs me tightly, tucking me further into his chest as we sway to the soft music. When we break apart, he leads me back to our table.

The rest of the night is uneventful. We stay half an hour longer before Julian makes our excuses. He seems quiet since we danced, which makes me wonder if I've done something wrong, but I'm unsure what. I'm probably overthinking it. We've had a nice evening and I felt like we connected well. He could be tired or something.

We walk back to the car in silence and I'm a little disheartened when he doesn't link onto my arm like he did on the way in. When we arrive back at the campsite, he holds the car door open for me.

"Well, I guess this is goodbye. Thank you for a beautiful evening," I say, feeling awkward. Something seems off balance.

"Goodnight, Kara." His tone is kind but I wish he'd say more.

When I turn to face the pod Toby, Lynne, and Alice are waiting for me on the deck. I hear the car pull away but I don't turn to wave.

"Did Cinderella enjoy the ball?" Lynne asks.

I try to look happy, even though I'm disappointed with how my night ended. I thought we shared a moment, but the way we left things said otherwise.

"Thank you. It was a wonderful night."

The girls help me out of my dress and we settle into some campfire games. I text my sister to tell her about Beatrice before I fall asleep on one of the deck chairs.

CHAPTER TWENTY FIVE

BEAR

"My inside source told me you were dancing with Kara last night," Vinnie says while fooling around on the deck. He holds his hands to the side of his face and makes flirty eyes at me. I shrug off his comment before going to help a family exit a swan. The morning is passing too slowly and the lake is now bare. Even the ducks are sunbathing on the banking. My phone rings for the fifth time, which I ignore.

"Come on, even you can admit she's easy on the eye," Vinnie says when the family head for the exit. He's not going to stop pushing until I give him something.

"She's a beautiful girl, okay? I admit it. Are you happy now?"

"I knew it!"

"Please. You know nothing," I say, rolling my eyes.

I don't usually show any interest in girls. It doesn't mean I'm going to act on my moment of weakness.

Kara returns with the morning drinks before Vinnie can question me further. She passes me a cup of coffee as my phone starts ringing again. With a groan, I pull it out of my pocket and head to the control room to take my dad's call. The door slams behind me as I enter.

"What's the problem?"

"Hello to you too. I'm calling to say well done on closing the deal with Beatrice."

"I don't know what you're talking about." My confusion echoes through my voice.

"I'm sorry I didn't tell you the truth, but I knew you could do it. Seeing you in action gave Beatrice the reassurance that we're the stable option. She's signing a five-year contract to focus on re-vamping the costumes in the park. I'm proud of you. You're stepping up your game."

I should be mad he's testing me. The truth is, I'm relieved I passed his scrutiny.

After saying goodbye, I end the call with my dad. I exit the control room, taking a drink of my coffee, and my gaze falls on Kara. She was amazing last night. She's probably the reason I won Beatrice's trust. She laughs at something Vinnie says. Her expression turns into a pretty smile when she sees me.

"What did I miss?"

"Vinnie thinks he's found my mystery hiding

place. Only he's not sharing the information. Personally, I think that means he has nothing."

"I wouldn't say I have nothing on you. I know your biggest secret," Vinnie teases.

"I could tell her a few of your stories," I say, relishing in the look of horror on his face.

"I'm not sure we have to go down that route." He laughs.

We both know he's proud of his drunken moments. They aren't secrets, although they would make Kara blush. He collects the paper cups when we finish our drinks and takes them to the bin on the main path.

"I'm sorry about Vinnie. When he gets an idea in his head, it's hard for him to let go."

"Don't worry about it. He's an interesting character. I like him just the way he is. Both of my teammates aren't so bad." She smiles playfully.

"I'm glad we're growing on you," I say with a smile.

"I think you've forgiven me for the mistakes of my first day too."

"You may be onto something there. It's quiet around here. Why don't you go for an early lunch? Vinnie and I can handle it here."

"Thanks, boss."

She salutes me, removes her lifejacket, and sets off down the deck. I shade my eyes to watch her leave.

Vinnie races towards me with a look of excitement on his face.

"Quick, close the ride before we miss her," he says.

"You can't be serious."

"Why? There's nobody on the lake, zero people waiting in the line, and this could be our only chance to catch her."

He reaches for the sign. I put my hand on it too as we stare each other down. This is silly. We should leave Kara to have her lunch in peace. Though, I must admit, I'm curious why this is such a big secret. Although, the hype is probably more exciting than the reality. She likes winding Vinnie up.

"Decide now or we're going to lose her."

Letting go of the sign, Vinnie puts it into place. We walk down the deck towards the staff changing room. Ducking behind the wall, we wait for Kara to come out. Once she has her lunchbox and a red checked blanket, she leaves the building, talking to Lynne.

"That's her big secret. She's having a tea party with the fairies. What a let-down. I'm going to get a sandwich from the van. I'll see you in an hour," Vinnie says with a heavy sigh.

I nod, setting my feet in motion towards my house. Vinnie takes off in the other direction. Keeping my distance, I fall into step behind Kara and Lynne. As Kara reaches the spot of our incident from the first day, she waves goodbye to Lynne, detouring into the trees. I can't resist following her. Why would this be her special place?

She unfolds her blanket before catching sight of me. Her hand covers her breast bone as she gasps.

"You scared me. What are you doing here?"

"This is your big secret? You like to sit and think about throwing me in the lake?"

"Don't be silly. That's not why I come here. This side of the lake is calming and peaceful. It's not the exact place we collided. The view here is pretty and I'm not usually disturbed. It's the perfect place to relax on a lunch break."

"I should go. I'm sorry for interrupting." I turn to leave.

"Julian."

At the sound of my name, I turn to find her directly behind me, and our eyes meet.

"Stay. Please."

My arm brushes against hers as she welcomes me onto the blanket. I lie beside her with my hands behind my head. She lies on her side, watching me.

"What do you do in this secret club?"

"It's not a club. There's only me and I usually read."

"Vinnie is going to be disappointed."

"You don't have to tell him you found me. That way he'll still think I'm cool."

I laugh. "You may be a lot of things, but in Vinnie's mind, cool is not one of them."

"What about you? Do you think I'm cool?" She playfully nudges me with her shoulder.

"Actually, I owe you a thank you. My dad rang earlier and he's managed to secure a business deal with Beatrice. I'm pretty certain you're the reason we won her over."

"That's great news, but I didn't do anything."

"You were a great date."

Kara's help means a lot to me. Having Beatrice on my side is a huge deal for me. She's a successful business women and a great asset. She's also kind and approachable when my dad's overbearing. Knowing she'll be on the team when I need her fills me with confidence. It's another step towards helping me take over the park.

"I'll have to take you to future events."

She smiles. "I'm a busy girl. I might not be free next time."

"You fight dirty. Maybe I should buy you flowers as a thank you."

"It's too late now. You've already told me about the gesture."

"I can come up with something else if you'd like."

She looks at my lips before averting her eyes. After a pause of silence, she sits up and looks out to the lake.

"Do you ever think about taking something that isn't yours?" I ask.

I run my palm through my hair. Her eyes meet

mine briefly before she looks away. I don't know what her deal is with Toby. Are they misunderstood friends who eventually will become more? Isn't that how it goes in the movies? Kara isn't mine, but it doesn't stop me from wanting her. *Would it be so bad to give in to an urge?* Our eyes meet again and she takes hold of my shirt, pulling me towards her.

"Like a stolen kiss, you mean?"

Before I can answer, her mouth comes crashing down on mine. Every nerve ending in my body comes alive. Her lips are warm and soft. The taste of apple and honey fills my senses as I drink her in. A kiss has never felt this good, and my hands stray up her back and into her silky hair. I can't get enough and I don't want this to end. She read my mind. This is exactly what I meant when I asked the question. Kissing Kara is like nothing I've experienced before. She's beautiful and delicious. Her touch is sweet and addictive. Kissing her is my undoing. I already want more. I already crave more.

CHAPTER TWENTY SIX

KARA

I'm kissing Julian. He's kissing me back. My pulse is racing and my heart feels like it's going to jump out of my chest. I've wanted to do this since I first met him back at the skate park at home. I'm taking a small taste of pure pleasure, a guilt-free moment of bliss, and I'm savouring every second of it.

Deep down I know it can't last. He said he isn't looking for a girlfriend, but that doesn't mean I can't steal a kiss or two. I just don't want him to reject me or say this can't happen again. As we break apart, doubt begins to creep in.

"Don't ruin the moment," I say, leaning back in towards him. I cover his lips again with mine.

Julian pulls me closer against his chest. His tongue dances with mine, full of passion and need. This is the perfect stolen kiss. It doesn't need to be analysed with words. My heart pounds with a new, desperate rhythm as heat washes over my skin. I nip at his bottom lip, his fingers tangle with mine, and my stomach flutters with butterflies. Initiating a red-hot kissing session is something I've never done before; Julian makes me want to take control. To seize what I need. He tastes of cherries and mint. He's addictive, delicious, and I can't get enough.

When we move apart, the spell of lust is broken. Our lunch break is over and I worry reality is about to kick in.

"We don't need to talk about this. Nobody has to know about it. This can be our secret." I bite my lip before continuing, "Unfortunately, we do need to get back to work though."

I try to act like this is no big deal. If I can keep our relationship causal, maybe this can happen again. I want more of Julian, and if that means keeping us a secret, I'm okay with it. The decision to kiss him was made on impulse. Now my brain has caught up, my words are calculated. I can handle a summer fling. I just need to keep my heart locked away.

Julian's face tightens, his emotions unreadable. I bite my fingernail, waiting for his response and hoping he doesn't tell me we can't do this again. He kisses my cheek, and I'm instantly relieved. He wants to continue whatever this is too.

I pull him to his feet and dust off my knees. All I need to do is act cool. This is no big deal. He helps me fold my blanket while our gazes stay locked on each other. His hand brushes against mine which sends a tingle down my arm. Unspoken words linger in the air and I wish I could read them.

On the way back to the changing room, we sneak glances at each other. My smile grows and Julian's sets firmly in place. I put my blanket and lunch box into my locker. When I arrive back at the deck, Julian's eating a burrito, watching me every so often.

When he disappears into the control room, Vinnie points at me.

"What did you do to him? He's been acting weird since he got back from lunch."

I shrug off his comment. "Me? Maybe it was you?"

He considers my answer and drops the subject. Now I'm wondering what he thinks he's done.

The afternoon passes as slowly as the morning. This is the quietest day in the theme park so far. Julian glances over at me intensely every few minutes. His emotionless expression stays in place.

I begin to doubt my actions. Kissing Julian probably wasn't my best idea. He isn't just some guy, he's my boss and a friend. He's someone special and way too good for me, while I'm just a small-town girl. If I'm lucky, I'll graduate university and find a good job. I'm not going to be a business tycoon or an inspirational role model. Dread settles in my stomach. I can't take it back and I'm not sure I want to, but what if I've made a mistake?

When the clock reaches five, I shoot off to my locker without a second glance at the guys. I need some time to think and calculate my next move. After quickly changing my clothes, I exit the building to find Julian leaning against the wall. A flicker of my flight response crosses my mind, but I decide against it.

Slowly, I approach him. "You're not going to fire me, are you?"

"Is that what you're thinking?" His frown deepens as his eyebrows knit together.

"You've barely spoken a word."

"I was giving you space."

"I was doing the same."

He pushes off the wall, coming to my side. We silently walk next to each other until we reach the woods. He keeps looking at me like he has something to say, yet the words never surface. From what I've learnt about him so far, he's either commitment-phobic or doesn't want a girlfriend to distract him. Kissing someone should be simple. Kissing Julian has only complicated things.

"I like you and I think you like me too," I say.

"Of course I like you..."

I interrupt him before he continues. This is my opportunity to set my terms before he tells me this can't work.

"I propose a summer romance. No serious feel-ings, just fun."

"Are you sure about this? I don't want anyone to get hurt."

If the concern on his face didn't look so genuine, I would roll my eyes. I can handle a causal relationship. It's not like I'm going to see him after the summer anyway.

"I can look after myself. Plus, I'm using you for your hot lips and party connections," I joke.

"Well, at least you're honest about it." He laughs, breaking the weird tension.

"I also think we should keep this between us two for now."

A scowl crosses his face; however, he nods in agreement. Does he want people to know about us? It's too late to ask now and we seem to be on the same page.

"Okay, missy. Now it's my turn to take control."

He walks towards me, backing me up against a tall, wide tree. Hunger fills his eyes like nothing I've seen before. His teeth nip at my bottom lip before we break into a full-blown tingling kiss. He rubs his hand over my cheek then into my hair. My skin is feverish from his every touch.

"You're cute when you demand I play by your rules. You need to remember you're in *my* world now. I'll keep us a secret, but I'll be taking kisses whenever I like. These beautiful pink lips are mine." He kisses me again, holding me in place. I just found a slice of heaven.

By the time I reach the pool, my lips are swollen and my hair is a mess. Looking in the mirror, my fingers trace my lips, remembering his touch. A smile settles on my face.

After showering, I sit on the small camp bed, brushing my hair. Helen's face appears on my phone. A high-pitched squeal makes me jerk away from the speaker.

"Kara, you're amazing. Ms. Finch wants me to mail some of my designs. She loves the samples I sent her today."

"Wait, back up a second. Who's Ms. Finch?"

"The lady from the dinner party you went to with Bear."

The cogs in my brain begin to turn. Julian is a distraction and I'm slow to hit the mark. "Beatrice?"

"Yes. She's very professional on the phone. This could be my big break." She giggles like an enthusiastic school girl.

"I'm happy for you. I want to know the second she calls you back."

"Of course. You'll be the first to know. I have to go or I'm going to be late for work, but thank you a million times!"

She ends the call and I flop back onto the bed, feeling content. My summer is working out perfectly. Footsteps on the creaky wood alert me to Toby's presence. He lingers in the doorway, trying to be quiet.

"You need new tricks. Your act is old," I say in a

monotone voice.

"It's a good job you've got an interview next week for the haunted house then."

"Wait, what?"

I sit up, turning too fast to face him and tumbling off the thin bed.

"Josh got the manager's job which means there's an opening. Our dreams of having the perfect summer together is about to get a jumpstart."

Toby holds his hand up, ready for a high five, and doesn't notice my hesitation. The unease in my stomach thickens as my hand meets his. He dances out of the room, grabbing his towel on his way. Sitting on the edge of the bed with my hands rested against my forehead, I ponder over my decision.

When Toby returns from the shower, we play a few rounds of blackjack with the cards and eat cheese toasties. I don't even know who's winning; my heart isn't in it. Toby does most of the talking, while I try to keep up, but honestly, I'm not listening half of the time.

That night, I struggle to sleep, knowing I have to disappoint one of my boys. Would Julian mind if I went to the interview? Maybe I wouldn't get the job anyway, but if I was offered it, would it be wrong to turn it down? Toby wants me close so we can have the summer we planned for. Whatever I do will be the wrong decision and the consequences could cost me everything.

CHAPTER TWENTY SEVEN

KARA

After a week of intense glances and wild kissing sessions, Julian and I have easily fallen into a pattern. He meets me for lunch and we've extended the walk back to the campsite. Vinnie has been watching us suspiciously, but he hasn't mentioned anything. I wouldn't care if he found out about us, but I'm not sure how Julian would feel about it. Today, I left the swan ride five minutes before Julian and he met me at the lake. He lies on the blanket. My palm grazes against his hard chest as I climb on top of him and our lips connect.

"You, Kara, are all kinds of beautiful."

"I'll admit you're a little yummy too."

He smiles. "You couldn't resist taking advantage of a sweet innocent boy like me."

"That's right. Corrupting you is my goal." I laugh against his neck.

He flips me onto my back, covering my lips with fiery kisses. There's nothing gentle about them. He's driving me crazy with every touch, like he knows which buttons to press. Lust bubbles to the surface as I allow my hands to wander over Julian.

"You've got me all wrong. Instigating the first kiss is a bold move, I'll give you credit for that, but you're the one who's in trouble." His words come out rough and flirty.

He grazes my stomach before gripping my thigh.

"I like the idea of being in trouble with you."

He licks and nibbles my ear as soft moans involuntarily leave my mouth. He sighs. "I'm afraid we've run out of time," he says.

I pout at his words. He helps me to my feet, stealing another soft kiss.

"To be continued," he adds as he squeezes my butt.

"Cheeky."

We exit our hideout and join the main path. I leave Julian outside the changing room and make my way inside.

Smoothing down my hair in the mirror, I return my things to my locker.

"A little whisper says you've got your eye on the dark woods."

My stomach fills with dread. I rub my forehead,

turning to face a colourful Lynne. "When Toby and I came here, we intended to spend every day together." I frown.

"So? What's the problem?"

My fingers tangle through my hair, which I tug to ease some of the tension. "There could be a new reason I don't want to move zones."

She holds her hands together, resting them on her shoulder in a classic sweetheart pose. "Could this have something to do with a guy?"

"It has everything to do with a guy. It's nothing serious and I'm not sure it will turn into more, but I don't want to hurt his feelings."

"You must do what your heart knows is true."

"Do they teach you these lines in fairy-tale school or were you born for the role?"

She laughs. "Honey, I'm just wise from a lifetime of mistakes. The way I see it is, if you don't follow your instincts, you'll always wonder *what if*."

This summer is about following the adventure and living in the now. I don't want to live with the regret of not doing what's right.

"I'm no closer to knowing what to do, but your advice is helpful. Thanks."

———

Deep, evil laughter fills the air as I hurry through the dark woods. I jump when the mummy rises from its tomb. After checking nobody is following me, I head for the dark lord's office. The park closed thirty minutes ago, and Antony is wearing his casual clothes. He invites me into his small room, moving a pile of papers off the chair so I can sit down.

"Sorry about the mess, I don't use this office much. Welcome to the place where everyday things go bump in the night. It's a little different from the fairy-tale world you're familiar with, although I think you'll like it here. Toby speaks very highly of you and I think you're going to fit in well."

I know how much Toby wants this for me. Us being together is how it's always been.

"He's a good friend."

He smiles. "I'll cut to the chase. The job's yours if you want it. We've a catalogue of costumes you're welcome to look through. You'll shadow someone for the first few days and can start as soon as Bear can free you up. It's that simple."

I cringe when I hear Bear's name. Telling Julian is going to be hard. My gut instantly fills with guilt.

"Does the costume determine where in the haunted house I'll be positioned?"

"Yes. Each room has a theme. There are many roles to choose from and you don't have to stick with just one. If we've got the outfit, it's yours to wear. There will be someone to help you with make-up and you no longer need to worry about sunblock." He laughs at his bad joke.

"I like working in the sun," I think out loud.

"You'll get used to the dark. Lunch breaks work on a rota, but you'll get an opportunity to take in a daily dose of Vitamin D." The idea of missing time with Julian deepens my frown. When I don't speak, he continues. "We're a big team. You'll have plenty of people to support you and help you settle in. All I need is for you to sign the transfer papers and we can wrap this up."

He sifts through a pile of dusty papers until he finds what he's looking for. The filing cabinet bangs as he pulls out a pen. Once he attaches them to a clipboard, he passes it to me. I stare at the paper before standing abruptly. The contract in my hand feels like I'm selling my soul to the devil. I like my little team and everything that goes with it.

"I'm sorry. I can't do this."

I stumble out of the tiny office before breaking into a run through the park. I feel safe once I'm in the woods surrounding the enchanted forest. Leaning against a tree, I catch my breath. Tonight was a mistake. Lynne was right; my heart belongs in the light. There's no dark path for me.

Toby is waiting for me outside the pod when I return home. His huge grin means his boss hasn't given him the news. He sets off party poppers when he sees me approach. Once I step onto the deck, he uncovers a confetti cannon. I hold my hands up, telling him to stop.

"I'm sorry. I couldn't do it."

"Do what? Did you go for the interview?"

"Yes." My voice cracks as my determination wavers.

"Then what's the problem? Antony gave you the job, right?"

"I choked. I couldn't go through with it." I cover my eyes with my hands, needing to block out his reaction.

"I don't understand. The haunted house isn't scary. The people inside will become your friends."

"It's not that; I like the sunlight and my team. Julian and Vinnie are both great guys and I want to stay with them."

His face turns red with anger as he begins to shout at me. "Julian. Since when did you start calling him that? Seriously, this is about someone you've known five minutes?"

"That's unfair."

Toby's double standards are starting to make my blood boil. The first sign of a girl showing interest and he would always bail on me. After all, Sophie is one of the reasons we are at Blue Oaks in the first place.

"I'll be a laughing stock tomorrow. I put myself out there for you," he rambles, passing me on the deck.

"I'm sorry. I'll make this up to you."

He runs his hands through his hair. "Don't bother."

He storms off without a second glance. By bedtime, he hasn't returned, which leaves me relieved. We both need time to cool off from our argument. When I unplug my phone from the charger, instead of texting him, I notice a message from an unknown number.

Night, beautiful.

My smile is instant.

How did you get this number?

I'm a stalker remember? I'm joking. It's in your work file.

Night, Julian. x

Sweet dreams, trouble ;).

CHAPTER TWENTY EIGHT

BEAR

The Perfect Storm is now my living movie. Okay, I'm exaggerating slightly. A full-blown gale is working up a storm, and there will be no lunchtime picnic for Kara and me. The ground is too wet. Rain is running down every pathway like a treacherous stream. My dad hasn't returned home yet which gives me overall responsibility of the park. Blue Oaks Theme Park has never shut its doors for anything other than the end of the season. Making an important decision like whether to close the park because of the weather is a lot of pressure. The loss in revenue will be high and I'm not sure how my dad will react to that.

A small group of park visitors run into the seating area which is covered with a canopy. Kara wipes the water from her face. She's drenched; we all are. Vinnie pulls his fallen hood back over his head.

The wind is loud; our conversations have been like a shouting match. The three of us have hardly spoken in the hour we've spent together. I brush the water from my face. I need to take control of this situation. Getting wet on the edge of the deck is only going to give us all a cold.

"If in any doubt, don't let anyone on the lake," I say.

"Who would want to go out there in this weather anyway?" Vinnie replies.

He has a point. I turn the sign over to close the ride. I don't want either of them to get ill because I left them outside in the rain.

"Both of you sit in the control room. I'm going to assess the park."

The wind and rain make it hard to talk. My voice comes out like I'm barking orders. The stress of having to make the final decision probably isn't helping either. I know what I need to do.

"Is your dad still not answering his phone?" Kara asks.

"He's probably in a meeting.

"Is there anything I can do to help?"

"No. I need to know you're safe. Stay with Vinnie and I'll be back soon."

"Stay safe."

I smile. I like that she's worried about me. I want to kiss her goodbye, but I resist, knowing Vinnie is watching us.

"I will. See you soon."

"Yes. See you soon."

———

Even with my thick parka on, I'm completely soaked. Heading into the gift shop, I borrow a disposable rain mac. I should at least send some of the staff with young families home, yet I'm hesitant.

Hurrying my pace, I make my way through the dark woods towards the park entrance. Antony waves me across when he catches sight of me. Taking shelter under the entrance, I wait to see what advice he offers.

"You're one lucky guy."

"How did you come to that conclusion?" I smooth down my dripping rain mac. We're not on the same page; he can't be talking about the weather. The rain doesn't seem to faze him, which I guess is the perk of working inside.

"Kara came for a transfer interview yesterday."

My lips tighten while my teeth grind together. His words are like a cold shower.

"She didn't mention anything."

"That's because her refusal took less than five minutes. She shot me down flat. What do your swans have that my haunted house lacks? Don't give me that bull story about the sun."

I unclench my jaw, feeling instant relief. All this

time I thought she had a secret crush on Toby. I was wrong. She chose to stay close to me. My grin stretches wide.

The sky lights up, bringing my attention back to the task in hand. I brush my hair out of my face. My relationship with Kara will have to wait.

"I need to go. Start sending people to the entrance. We need to close the park down."

He gives a sharp nod. Thunder rumbles in the sky as I take off running. The main entrance isn't much farther. Penny is sitting in the blue admissions office, typing on her keyboard. She looks up when I tap on the glass window.

"Am I glad to see you," she says.

"We need to close the park. The weather is getting out of hand. My dad isn't answering his phone so I'm making the call."

"I'll send out the announcement now. What shall I tell the people who complain?"

"Give them free tickets or put them up in the hotel. Either way, I want everyone out of here."

I don't care about people's complaints. I just want to make sure everyone is safe.

The wind is picking up. Lightning flashes, and the thunder crashes loudly. Picking up the master radio, I send a code red message out to all staff in the park, telling them to start the evacuation. Penny grabs the check-in register and begins talking people out of the park. Once she has the situation under control, I head back to my team. The water is deep and my ankle boots are filling up. People pass me on their way out and I offer help where I can.

Kara and Vinnie are standing in the gift shop with the rest of the staff when I return. I hand out rain macs to anyone who will take them. Vinnie helps himself to a handful of sweets with a cheeky grin which I wave off.

"Is the enchanted forest clear?" I ask.

"All clear," someone shouts from the back. I radio to the other nine zones in the park, receiving the same message. After checking back with Penny, I hand over my responsibilities to the security team. Lockdown of the park is almost complete, and I can breathe more easily.

"It's time we all get out of here."

"This sucks as a free holiday," Vinnie says.

"Think yourself lucky you're not heading back to the campsite," Kara says out loud.

"You're coming with me," I say to her, trying not to draw too much attention to my words. To the group, I shout, "The hotel is open to anyone who needs a room. Penny in the admissions office is the person to see. Let's go, everyone."

Once back at the house, I leave Kara to use my en-suite as I send the housekeeping staff home to be with their families. My heart is pounding from the adrenaline of taking charge of the park. The water in my socks squelches against the carpet. Using the main bathroom, I have a quick shower, then change into my tracksuit bottoms and a t-shirt. I grab a tall glass of milk and sit at the kitchen counter, trying to calm my nerves. My phone vibrates against the marble top, alerting me to an incoming call from my father. I hesitate, wondering how my dad is going to react to my decision. I look out of the window to see the storm isn't letting up and I stand by my choice. Hitting the green button, I pull the phone to my ear.

"Is everyone safe? I couldn't leave the meeting once it got started. The news is suggesting major floods in most parts of England." My dad sounds worried.

"I've shut down the park," I say bracing myself for his reaction.

"Thank the heavens. I'm proud of you for using your initiative."

I let out a sigh of relief as I relax into my seat. Smoothing down my hair, the tension leaves my body. Once I end the call, my gaze catches Kara standing in the doorway. She's wearing one of my skater t-shirts, and I like seeing her in my clothes.

"Sorry. I didn't want to interrupt. You did a great job today."

Her proximity fills me with warmth. Her soft, wet hair smells good as I bury my head into her neck. Kara's arms heat my skin as she wraps them around me. This feeling in my chest is foreign; I'm not used to having someone care about me. My previous relationship never felt like this and Kara isn't even mine. She's holding all the cards and I feel off-balance because I don't think she likes me as much as I like her. She said she only wants something meaningless. The thing is, I'm free-falling fast and I don't know how to stop. Kara and I are getting along really well, and I'd like more of her time, even if she doesn't want a relationship.

"Why did you decide to stay with me instead of moving across the park to be with Toby?"

Kara's body stiffens against mine. "You heard about that. I like working with you and Vinnie. We may not be scaring people, but we make our own entertainment."

"So, it's Vinnie and me you're sticking around for?"

"Yes. You're my boys." She pats me on the back before walking to the fridge. "Let me whip you something to eat up for your hard work today."

I give a small smile. I'm not going to lie to myself; her words hurt a little. I want her to want me, only me.

I watch her in action, chopping and dicing vegetables. A couple of eggs and a sprinkle of pepper later, and I'm looking at a perfect veggie omelette.

"Service with a kiss. One Kara special."

She places the plate in front of me, lightly kissing me on the lips, and goes to make her own lunch. Sitting opposite me on the stool, she licks her lips in anticipation.

"This is something."

Her smile beams at my compliment. "It's Hayley and Anna's favourite. The girls have me making these whenever I look after them."

"I can see why. What other magic can you work?"

She nervously laughs, raising her eyebrows.

Thirty minutes later, we're snug on the sofa, eating chilli chocolate and custard pots while watching *Spiderman*. A moan leaves my mouth when the taste zings on my tongue. Kara playfully dips the spoon into her dish and smears it onto my face.

Laughing, I say, "I'm sorry but I won't be retaliating. This is way too good to waste."

"Who said anything about not eating it?"

She licks the side of my face and I steal a hot, passionate chocolate kiss.

"I'm labelling this my new favourite dessert."

She kisses my cheek and snuggles into my side.

CHAPTER TWENTY NINE

KARA

Soft feathers glide over my skin as I wrap myself deeper into the warm cocoon. The beautiful male spooning me smells of mint and sweet cherries. I breathe him in, not wanting to wake from this pleasant dream.

Gentle, addictive kisses flutter up my arm onto my collarbone. Every single one tingles in my core. I could stay like this forever. In my wildest fantasies, I never knew I could feel so alive.

"I have to get up. Sweet dreams," Julian whispers in my ear as the reality of where I am heightens my senses.

My eyes slowly open to find his handsome face staring at me. His expression holds a hint of something I can't place.

"Sorry I woke you. It was greedy of me, but I needed one last taste before I have to leave."

Warmth fills my chest. "It s a sweet way to be woken up and I don't mind at all."

He kisses me gently at first, each intoxicating touch adding to the fire growing inside me. I desperately want more as he deepens the kiss.

"Sorry to be a buzzkill, but I do need to go. We can pick this up later." He speaks as he breaks away.

He places a peck on the top of my head before rolling off the bed.

Watching Julian navigate around his own space is mesmerising. I can't help stealing glances at his body as he dresses into his uniform. Flinging back the covers, I rise from the most comfortable bed in the world.

"I'm coming with you."

"It's not even seven a.m. and I have to meet with the health and safety team. It's going to be boring. I have to listen to the risk assessment report before I can open the park. Why don't you stay here and I'll bring breakfast back with me."

"As tempting as that may sound, I want to see where the magic happens."

"If this was a movie, this would be where I say a cheesy pick-up line like the magic happens where you slept last night."

A warm blush rises up my cheeks, heating my face. Last night barely made an age fifteen rating, but I can't help my flush exterior. Julian is the perfect gentleman.

My clean clothes are waiting for me on a chair outside the bedroom door. Dressing quickly, I meet Julian in the kitchen. With a piece of toast in hand, we walk out the door, heading straight for the theme park. It's cold and the ground is wet, but at least it's not raining. Already, I miss the luxury of the warm bed. Returning to the campsite is going to be painful.

Julian was right; the meeting is long and dull. It's too early to take in the risk and damage assessment. Instead, I focus on the important bit. The park will open as usual, although the lake water level is too high. The boats will stay out of order. We'll need different jobs for the day.

"I hope this isn't a mistake on my part, but why don't you join Toby in the haunted house? Delegating you to Antony makes sense. He needs the help and I want to know you're safe. I just hope you don't have too much fun."

"Being inside on a cold day sounds like a good idea to me."

Also, it'll be good for me to see Toby. I'll be able to apologise for our argument. We never stay mad at each other for long. Me not working with him is going to be confusing and won't help my case, but hopefully he can see things from my point of view. I'm settled at my swan ride and I don't have to do everything with him.

I pull Julian into a sizzling kiss. The last twelve hours have been amazing, and he's making me want more than a summer fling. Having my own future instead of being the supporting act feels within my grasp.

———

The haunted house has a cold draught which gives me goose pimples and causes a shiver to run down my spine. My outfit resembles an evil fairy godmother and smells like fake cherries. Sophie sticks the last few gems to my face and points to the mirror.

"How do I look?" I say, spinning around.

"You'll fit in perfectly between the bad apples in the rotten tea party. Lynne will be proud."

She snaps a picture to send to her which makes me smile widely. Sophie's my acting mentor for today and I'm enjoying spending time with her. My dress is purple and black, and I look like a broken fairy. We look similar other than our colours. Sophie's outfit is blue and red. The fake blood, ruby red glitter, and dusty cobwebs on my face make me look badass.

"Now all we need is to master your cackle and we're good to go."

She braces her stance, holding her fingers out wide. She clears her throat, getting into character.

"Eyebrows down, wonky smile, evil hands, throw

your head back, and let out a high-pitched hysterical laugh."

She sounds like something out of a horror movie as her laugh ripples like an evil villain's. When she breaks character, my frozen expression loosens into a nervous giggle. Taking a deep breath, I follow her lead and let out a crazy laugh. Heat warms my cheeks; I feel a little silly doing this.

Sophie wraps her arm around my shoulders, leading me into the haunted house. "Come on. We need to get into position. We can work on the cackle."

Toby catches a glimpse of me and does a double-take. He pauses for a split second before disappearing down a secret passage. He's clearly still mad at me.

The music starts, signalling there is a presence within the house. My pulse quickens as my nerves kick in; I might not be cut out for scaring. The hairs on the back of my neck stand up as a chill passes through my body. Sophie grabs my hand, pulling me into the broken teacup prop. She points at the dim spotlight above our head, instructing me to wait for the right moment. Screams echo around the house as the sound of glass breaking and chains rattling fill the air.

The bright spotlight beams down on us as we stand on cue. My cackle comes out strong while the children run through the room. Robotic worms wiggle on a nearby plate and the people scurry out as fast as they can. Sophie grabs my arm as her laughter turns pleasant.

"I knew you could do it!" she says excitedly.

"That was fun."

"It's almost as good as squeezing Toby's firm bum."

Gross. I don't need to hear about Toby's intimate relationship. "That's way too much information. Are things going well with you guys?"

"He's sulking at the moment, though that has more to do with you than me. Toby and I are more than friends which is working out perfectly."

I hold my hands up to stop her giving any more details and she swats them away. "He's like a brother to me. It's just wrong knowing about his love life, but I'm happy for you both."

She gives a mischievous grin and hugs me. "You two will make up when he realises why you didn't choose to join us, although you being here today will have him in a head spin."

I'm not sure for what reason she thinks I chose not to join this team, but I don't enlighten her. Talking to Toby will set my world back on its axis. The only thing is, even by dinner, I'm struggling to track him down.

CHAPTER THIRTY

KARA

The contagious grin on Julian's face as he walks towards me fills me with excitement. I tuck my hair behind my ear, joining him on the nearby path as Sophie waves goodbye to me. The dazzle in her eyes says she knows our secret. I guess it isn't that hard to work out. My hand automatically reaches out for Julian, but I disguise the gesture by rubbing my fingers over my arm.

"I hope you didn't miss me too much," Julian says.

"Sophie is cool, I've enjoyed hanging out with her. My day's been good, although I've missed my team." I nudge him playfully with my elbow.

"Hopefully everything will be back to normal by tomorrow."

We smile at each other. My gaze drops to his lips and his eyes darken.

"Do you want to sleep over tonight?" he says huskily.

I hesitate before answering. I'm glad he wants me to hang out with me and I like where our relationship is heading. Being with Julian is what I want, but it's also the easy option.

"I would love to spend the night with you, but I should find Toby. He's avoiding me and I need him to forgive me."

"Why did you fall out?" He presses his lips tightly together.

"Nothing you need to worry about. A night back at the campsite and we'll be the best of friends again."

Walking across the watery grass feels like quicksand. My shoes fill like holey buckets. The pod is an island within the mess. Julian helps me onto the deck, even though his boots must be filling up too. He brushes a strand of hair from my face before kissing me softly on the lips.

"Are you sure you want to stay here? You might like pool parties, but this is something else. It doesn't even look like Toby's home."

The place is in darkness with the curtains drawn. I kiss him gently on the lips, allowing my hand to linger on his cheek.

"Sophie told me he slept here last night. He'll return home eventually. It's cute you're worrying about me though."

We kiss again, but this time it carries some heat. I could easily get lost in Julian.

"I want to ask you something," I say.

I lean back so I can look into his eyes. I'm nervous about what I'm going to ask, but I want to know where I stand. I'm starting to like Julian and I want to know if he feels the same way.

"So this is why you ditched me," Toby interrupts from behind me.

I jump away from Julian like I caught fire. It's a mixture of nerves and shock that make me overreact. I don't know how Julian feels about Toby knowing about us and I wanted to talk to him first.

"You're home," I say, wanting to smack my forehead for stating the obvious.

"I spent all night worrying about you. Why didn't you message me?"

His nostrils flare. I've given Toby another reason to be angry with me. We need to talk about our fight before our argument gets out of control.

"A lot of things were going on and I forgot. I'm sorry."

"I bet," he says, folding his arms across his body while thrusting out his chest. His face reddens with anger.

Turning to Julian, I caress his wrist. "I'll see you tomorrow," I whisper.

He looks like he wants to say something. Instead, he kisses my temple before tackling the muddy water.

Toby doesn't seem to notice the swamp as he storms toward me.

"You know who he is, right?"

He points at Julian like he wishes he was holding a sword.

What the hell has gotten into him?

"Of course I do. He's an amazing person inside and out. Once you get to know him, he'll win you over too. Don't worry about my relationships."

"Guys like him will say anything to get you into bed." He spits the words out like venom.

The vein in his forehead pulses angrily. Usually I'd try to soothe his temper, but his words are making my blood boil. I can take care of myself.

"You don't know what you're talking about. Let's not argue. I just want to get back to being friends. I'm sorry I'm being a little selfish, but isn't that why we're here, to have fun?"

"This summer is about us having fun *together*. You swanning off with lover boy isn't what I had in mind."

"That's not what's happening. I didn't choose to leave you. Plus, we both know the first sign of a girl and you'd leave me without a second glance. Your date with Sophie on our day off proves my point."

"That's not fair."

"It's true though."

We both know I'm right. He thinks for a moment before he speaks again.

"I don't want to fight with you."

"I don't want to fall out either."

He stretches his arms out in front of him. "What do you say to macaroni cheese with a strawberry milk-shake for tea?"

I sigh with relief. "That sounds like a camping feast. It doesn't get much better than my best friend and a favourite meal."

I smile, trying to be positive. Breaking the tension will hopefully help him forgive me.

In perfect harmony, we work the camp stove, preparing the tinned food. Sitting in front of the small wind-up heater, we eat our macaroni cheese using disposable forks. We wave at Alice as she trudges past in her bright red wellingtons. On the surface, mine and Toby's relationship appears to be back on track, yet I can sense his mood is still bitter.

"How come you didn't go to the hotel last night?" I ask.

"I like it here."

"Come on, Tobes. Forgive me."

I lightly kick his foot. When he doesn't crack a smile, I do my best cat impression, rubbing my head up and down his arm like he's catnip. A hint of a smile plays on his lips.

"Come here."

He wraps his arms around me, hugging me tightly. He can't stay mad at me for long. Toby kisses the top of my head and I return his tight squeeze, locking my hands behind his back.

CHAPTER THIRTY ONE

BEAR

Placing a cup of coffee in front of my dad, I lean against the counter. He doesn't look up from his papers. His pen scribbles across the page as he pushes his glasses back up to the bridge of his nose. His workload is crazy busy after the trip.

"Can I help you with anything?" I ask, sipping my coffee.

He finally looks up like he's only just seen me. He throws his pen onto the table in frustration.

Taking a mouthful of the hot coffee, he lets out a sigh. "Thank you for the offer, but I have everything under control. It's going to take a few days to get back on track, but thanks to you, my job is easier."

"Anyone would've done the same thing." I shrug.

"Don't do that. I give credit where it's due; you did me proud."

My heart swells to hear his words and I fight to suppress my smile. He rises from his chair, embracing me in a hug and patting me on the back. We have a moment of pure understanding for the first time since the glimpse I got on graduation day. Following in my father's footsteps is my legacy, and these baby steps give me the confidence I need. Maybe I *can* do this.

He places two slices of bread into the toaster, pressing down the handle. "Do you want some?"

Checking my watch, I say, "Sorry, I've got to go."

I make it into the forest to meet Kara a few minutes later than usual. Toby comes barrelling towards me, diverting from his usual route. His nostrils flare as he invades my personal space.

"She's already gone." His lips curl in distaste.

"I'll catch her up. There's no reason to overreact." I keep my voice calm.

He steps closer.

"I'm not overreacting. Neither of you had the decency to let me know she was safe during the storm."

"I'm sorry we had you worried. She was with me; she's safe with me."

He shakes his head. "I'm the one who looks after Kara," he says sternly.

"What's your problem?"

"You're a complication Kara doesn't need. She isn't a toy you can throw away."

Is he for real? Toby is Kara's best friend, but he doesn't know me. Of course she isn't a plaything.

"I know how special she is. I would never use her."

He jerks his head up, gazing into my eyes with a murderous glare. "Kara's looking for her soulmate, her true match. She deserves only the best. You, buddy, don't have the qualities to keep a girl like her." He prods my chest with his bony finger.

"What, and you do?" The muscles in my arms tense as my anger begins to rise.

"I know her better than you. If you care for her at all, you should do the right thing and set her free before it's too late."

He may be her best friend, but I'm finding it hard to restrain myself. Kara and I had never spoken about where our relationship could lead. When she suggested a summer romance, it wasn't what I wanted. I wanted to give us a chance to see what this was between us. I originally thought her relationship with Toby was leading to something more than friends, but every opportunity Kara has had, she's chosen me. Is he angry because he has secret feelings for her, or is he being protective of his friend?

"I do care about her. I wouldn't intentionally hurt Kara." I say.

"How do you see this ending? She isn't part of your world. Taking her to fancy parties and filling her head with big dreams isn't what she needs. Kara is a traditional girl with family values. She needs to be with people who love her. She came here to have a little fun. You're setting her up for heartache."

Toby's words don't add up. An everlasting relationship is the last thing Kara said she wants from me.

"My relationship with Kara is none of your business."

"Who do you think will pick up the pieces when you mess up? Kara and I are family. You're a disaster waiting to happen. End this fling now before it gets out of hand." He uses his elbow to jostle me out of the way as he passes in a cloud of rage.

He's her best friend. Could his words carry some truth? Kara is a unique, beautiful girl. I don't want to hurt her. The future I can offer isn't for everyone. My life is here in the park. After university, there will be no long charity trips or lengthy holidays. I'll be here almost all of the time. That will never change, but it doesn't mean I have to tie Kara here too. Suppressing whatever her dreams are isn't my intention. I don't want to hold her back. I've already seen a glimpse into how close Kara is with her family. I wouldn't want to keep her away from them. I can't move to Northumberland, I'm anchored to Blue Oaks. As much as I hate it, Toby *is* looking out for his friend. He's right; I can't give her everything she deserves.

I find Kara standing by the lake, looking out into the water while she waits for me. Her face brightens with a smile as I approach. My emotions are too raw to keep my face in anything other than a tight grimace.

"Are our swan boats back open today? I'm missing my boys."

Her sweet voice breaks with emotion as my own turns into a growl. "You should stay with Toby in the haunted house."

She's a smart girl; the car crash that's about to happen already shimmers in her eyes. Nevertheless, she continues.

"Oh, is it going to take another day for the water to settle down?"

"The haunted house is a better fit for you." I grit my teeth. I hate myself already and I can't think clearly.

"What's wrong with you?" She seems confused rather than angry.

"It would be best if we cool things down. Take some time to adjust. We agreed that nobody should get hurt and I need some space to think about what I want. My position in the park is going to develop and take up all of my free time. You need to concentrate on your family and education. We aren't on the same page."

Anger flares in her eyes as her gaze follows the ghost of her best friend's steps. "Did Toby say something to you? I saw him leave the woodlands before you arrived."

"He wants what's best for you. I can't give you

everything you deserve. That much is clear." My voice starts to waver. Being cruel to be kind is not who I am and pain builds in my chest like a stone crushing my lungs.

"Toby doesn't understand this. He needs to get to know you. With time, he'll like you as much as I do. Please give us a chance." She reaches out towards me, but pulls her hand back before making contact.

Toby has made it clear he doesn't like me around Kara. They may not have romantic feelings toward each other, but whatever is going on between them isn't something I want to be mixed up with. His words play in my mind 'You, buddy, don't have the qualities to keep a girl like her.'

"I'm sorry, Kara."

The ache in my heart almost brings me to my knees as a tear rolls down her face. What have I done? I reach for her, but she knocks my hand away.

"I can't believe this is happening. You and Toby are both the same. I can make my own decisions; I don't need either of you to interfere."

She takes off running into the forest. I should follow her, but Toby's words hold me back. My mistake was allowing her to get close. Letting her go is my only option to save us both. My legs feel like jelly as I walk away. I rub the back of my neck, trying to comfort myself.

Vinnie's waiting for me when I reach the boats. The beauty of the lake now seems dull. None of it means very much if it reminds me of the one thing I can't have.

"I'm taking the day off to be with my dad. I'll find someone to work with you."

Backing away from the dock, I break into a sprint. I don't stop until my lungs are about to burst. Regret fills my heart; Kara means more to me than anyone ever has. It's selfish of me to want her, and now I'll never know if she could love me regardless of my anchor to the theme park. I've ruined everything.

CHAPTER THIRTY TWO

KARA

Throwing my clothes in a bag is the easy part as I hardly brought anything with me. I don't bother to fold them. I screw them into a ball like the tight mechanism of my broken heart. Getting out of here can't happen fast enough.

The train leaves in thirty minutes. I have plenty of time to pack but there's no way I want to miss it. The farther away from this place I can get, the better. The thought of seeing Julian or Toby again fills me with anger. Their betrayal of my trust stings like a sharp thorn in my side as neither one of them valued my opinion. I should give Toby a piece of my mind. How dare he interfere with my relationship? And why did Julian listen to him? The reasons he gave me for wanting space didn't make sense. We were fine this morning; our relationship was becoming something more. I could feel it.

Dragging my suitcase through the mud, I don't look back at the pod. The direction I'm walking is not the way to the train station. I need to return my keys and I need to know why Toby did this. As I enter the haunted house, Antony moves out of my way. My murderous glare burns into him as I push my suitcase towards him abandoning it against the wall. We don't speak. My hands are shaking with rage and he seems to understand. I move through the staff passageway, missing out most of the house. Toby had his zombie costume laid out this morning so I know where to find him. I ignore the zombie approaching me. It's not who I'm looking for. The purple light creates outlines of people rather than showing their features. Normally I'd find this unnerving as the costumes are scary, but I can't think of anything other than finding my target.

I recognise Toby immediately. The way he moves, and the tone of his voice, are as familiar to me as my own family. He's supposed to be my best friend. I thought I knew him as well as I knew myself. I was wrong. The person in front of me feels like a traitor, not a friend. He moves closer. Unlike me, he doesn't seem to realise who I am. His arms graze my shoulders. Without thinking, I push him away.

"What the hell did you say to Julian?" The fury I feel coats my words.

He stumbles back. "Kara. What I said was for your own good. He's not right for you."

The light flashes and I can see he's regained his balance.

"How would you know what's right for me? I thought we understood each other after our conversation last night." I throw my hands up in the air. The purple light shines in my eyes.

"He's a billionaire. You're nothing more than a game to him. He isn't going to fall for a small-town girl. People like us work for what we have, it isn't handed to us. You should date someone with similar goals." His voice is raised like he's angry which only provokes my own irritation.

I take a step back. "So that's what you think? I'm not worthy of someone because they have money. You make it sound like I'm not capable of making up my own mind. I thought we were friends, or did I misunderstand that too?" My words come out strong and I'm determined not to back down.

He moves towards me, but I hold my arms up, hoping he can see me well enough to stop.

"I love you like a sister and I was trying to stop you getting hurt. Talking about him last night made me realise you were blind to what was happening."

He has a funny way of showing he loves me. My heart is hurting more than ever before.

"It's too late for you to stop me getting hurt. *You*

did this. I've lost the guy I was falling for and my best friend."

He slumps his shoulders. "Don't say that. We can fix this. You don't need Julian. We were great before he came into the picture."

His words are raw but he doesn't understand how much I wanted my time with Julian. It doesn't matter if I got hurt in the end. It was my relationship, my choice.

"I can't be your sidekick for the rest of my life. I was going to find someone eventually."

"I know you were, but I didn't want it to be so soon."

I can't believe the words he's saying.

"It's okay for you to date, but not me. You're selfish, you know that?"

"Sorry for not wanting to lose my best friend for the summer to someone who doesn't deserve her."

"You don't know anything about Julian. You didn't bother to get to know him. I'm done with this."

I can't take any more of his excuses. I throw the keys at him and get the hell out of here. My hands begin to shake again. I'm furious. Helen told me he's self-absorbed many times before and I never believed her. But I've never wanted anyone like I want Julian, so playing the supporting role to Toby and his life has never felt like a problem before now.

I could scream.

After collecting my suitcase, I make my way to the

station. I can't wait to be home with my family. I arrive in the nick of time to see the train roll onto the platform and I hurry to take a seat in a half-empty carriage. The second my back hits the seat, I let out a huff. I slump down into the seat. The man opposite me gives me a strange look, but I don't care. I'm going home. As the train pulls out of the station, my breathing settles into an easier rhythm. I watch my nightmare summer fade into the background. The beautiful countryside allows me to escape my unpleasant thoughts.

Once the familiar view of my hometown is in sight, my anger is a distant memory. Instead, I feel numb with confusion.

Why would Toby ruin this for me? Julian cares for me, I know it. It hurts to think he could cast me aside so easily; the whole mess is better forgotten. Now I can go to university with a clear head. No longer in Toby's shadow, I can find my own friends; focus on my experiences and making memories. I would never hold Toby back, but he doesn't always consider my feelings. Now he won't have to because I'm done being the nice girl. The silver lining to my summer is the confidence to be me. Lynne, Vinnie, and even Sophie all like me for being myself.

———

The exterior of the house looks the same as when I left. I take a few seconds to study the detail. The summer breeze fills my nose with the scent of wild-flowers instead of machinery and dirt. I inhale deeply, welcoming myself home.

The front door closes behind me with a loud bang as I fall over my bag. I curse under my breath. Thick mud decorates my ankles. My shoes are falling apart, and the grass stains grazing my thighs give the impression I've been rolling in the dirt rather than camping. I run my fingers through the tangles in my hair, stopping mid-length when I notice something unexpected.

"What's going on in here? It looks like you've brought your work home with you." I can't hide my surprise to see our kitchen table full.

Helen looks up from her vintage sewing machine with a curious smile on her face. Her reading glasses rest on the end of her nose. Beatrice holds up the project they're working on with pride. The vibrant colours almost glow in the light.

"Your sister is a hidden treasure." Her voice is warm and kind.

Forgetting my dirty bag and water-leaking suit-case, I step into the kitchen to find a mountain of homemade designs. I'm surrounded by Helen's talented work. My hand runs over the beautiful fabric, admiring her craft.

"What happened to you? You're filthy. I should've made this waterproof overnight bag before you went away. It has a fold-up rain mac inside and it looks like you could've used it," Helen says.

"I love it. Campers everywhere will be lining up to buy them, however, I'd be happy never to go back there again. Didn't you guys experience the crazy British weather?"

"We had a thunder storm but I didn't realise your pod wasn't up to scratch. You're my inspiration for my new project. I'm so happy you like them."

"When Helen sent me the design, I couldn't resist meeting her. We've been working on the waterproofs ever since." Beatrice smiles.

"That's fantastic. What about your job?" I ask with concern.

"Beatrice has me under contract. *This* is my job now."

At least I got something right this summer.

"Where are Hayley and Anna?"

"Out with their dad, but they should be back soon." Helen sits up straighter, looking me in the eye. "So, really... what are you doing here?"

Of course she would want more information about why I was back, and in such a mess. She was my big sister, after all. She always knew when something was wrong, even if I really didn't want to talk about it.

"It's a long, complicated story."

"Boy trouble?" they say in unison.

I wave off their assumption. "Something like that."

"He doesn't deserve a good friend like you. He puts himself first way too often," Helen says.

I don't need to tell Helen what happened for her to presume it involves Toby. I knew she'd come to this conclusion. Usually, I'd shake off her comment, disagree with her logic. I hesitate for a second too long and Beatrice is the one to answer.

"He's a caring soul. He's always putting other people first. It must be a misunderstanding."

"How do you know Toby?" Helen asks Beatrice with a frown.

"Who's Toby? I'm talking about Julian," Beatrice asks.

They both look at me in confusion as I run my palm through my knotty hair and down the back of my neck.

"Toby is my best friend. Julian is the boy I like, or did like. I'm not sure anymore. They're both on my hit list."

I fill them in on my situation over a cup of tea while they take a break from sewing.

"The way Julian looked at you, I could tell he had strong feelings. He's not the sort of boy to enter into something lightly." Beatrice tells me.

"It doesn't matter. It's over now."

———

I help in the kitchen for the remainder of the afternoon. Helen pushes the material through the machine. I pass zips and buttons, while Beatrice outlines patterns with chalk.

"What's this suitcase doing here?" one of the twins shouts as I hear shuffling in the hall. Cringing, I realise I've forgotten to move my things. The girls freeze in the doorway as they see me. Their mouths are wide open like they've forgotten how to speak. Hayley is the first to squeal before they race towards me, knocking the wind from my lungs as they hug me tightly.

"I've missed you while I've been away," I say.

"There's so much we need to tell you. We've had our ears pierced and Anna has try-outs for drum lessons. She wants to be in a band," Hayley says.

I haven't spoken to them much in the last couple of weeks. My absence gives me a new sense of loss. I could've spent my time with my loved ones.

"Hayley has a newspaper round," Anna says.

"I can't imagine you getting out of bed early."

I offer a teasing smile.

"A girl's got to do what a girl's got to do." Hayley sighs dramatically.

"She wants some designer shoes." Anna screws up her face in distaste.

"Why do you need expensive footwear?"

"All the popular girls will have them." Hayley shrugs like my question was silly.

"Just promise me you'll still be yourself when you start high school."

"Of course. Being unique is the new cool, but I still need the shoes. Tell us about your trip and don't spare any details."

"I've been a wicked fairy, raced around the lake in a paddleboat, learnt to skateboard, and toasted marshmallows under the stars. It's been a blast."

"Were there any cute boys?" Hayley looks too interested in the answer.

"We know there was at least one," Anna adds with a smirk.

"Maybe," I say, trying to look happy with a false smile.

My phone rings from my pocket, and I automatically pull it out. The screen lights up with a picture of me and Toby hugging. Neon paint glows from our faces. My smile fades. Clicking the ignore button, I leave my phone on the kitchen counter.

"Come on. Let's go watch a movie."

CHAPTER THIRTY THREE

KARA

The soft duvet almost makes me forget where I am. My eyes slowly open, unveiling the reality of the small office. The scent of bacon tantalises my nostrils and my mouth waters. Placing my feet on the floor, I rise from the bed. A quick splash of water on my face and I'm ready to go downstairs.

Entering the kitchen, I find my family preparing the morning food. All signs of sewing materials are missing from view. Derrick flips omelettes in the frying pan. Anna puts crumpets into the toaster, while Hayley pours the glasses of orange juice. Helen races around the kitchen, setting up the cutlery. Everyone smiles when they see me.

"What can I do?" I ask.

"Take a seat, sleepyhead. We've got everything under control," Helen says.

I smooth down my hair.

"Toby's been calling your phone, although I think your battery is almost dead. The vibrations almost knocked your phone onto the floor. I had to push it back before it fell off," Anna says.

My attention flickers to the kitchen counter where I'd left my phone on purpose overnight. I push down all thoughts of reviving it. I don't want to reconnect with the outside world. I'm still annoyed with Toby. Avoiding him is sensible, so I don't say something I'll later regret.

"What's everyone doing today?" I ask, hoping to spend some time with my family.

"I'm sewing more weekend bags as soon as breakfast is over."

"We're going to the swimming club," the girls say in unison.

"The garden is my project today. It's overgrowing like a jungle," Derrick says.

I'm disappointed nobody is free to hang out with me. A sharp knock at the door interrupts my thoughts. I'm not sure where I fit into everyone's plans. The parcel from the postman is heavy and I struggle to bring it inside. Helen rubs her hands together.

"My new fabrics are here," she cheers.

"Breakfast first, Helen, before you start to get lost in your work," Derrick scolds.

She pouts before smiling. Helen kisses Derrick on

the cheek, taking her seat at the table. Derrick fills the plates with bacon while Anna piles up the crumpets.

"Where are you going today?" Anna asks me.

"I have no plans yet."

"Jordan has been asking about you."

I roll my eyes. "I've had enough of boys to last me until Christmas."

Beatrice swarms into the kitchen, the sound of the door shutting echoing in the background.

"Has our delivery arrived?"

Helen points at the brown paper parcel and Beatrice's eyes brighten. Helen abandons the food on her plate and washes her hands in the sink. They take off into the living room, giggling with excitement. Derrick shakes his head, although he doesn't try to stop her this time.

"You're welcome to help me in the garden if you're looking for something to do, Kara," Derrick says.

"Thanks. I might take you up on that offer."

"Don't do it! He's a slave driver," Anna says, laughing.

"You didn't even last an hour before you got distracted." Derrick laughs.

"I rest my case." Anna says as Derrick ruffles her hair.

Two hours later, dirt is under my fingernails and I have a bucket full of weeds. Derrick plants small trees, covering the freshly dug soil, and the garden is looking much healthier.

"I've asked your sister to marry me." It's hard to read his tone. He seems to be waiting for my reaction. I pause after throwing a dandelion into the bucket. I should've guessed something was on his mind when he asked me to help.

"Oh yeah? What did she say?"

"She hasn't given me an answer yet."

"When did you ask her?"

"About a week ago. She said she needed time."

"Good luck. I know things have been difficult, but she seems happy now."

"I think you're right. I love her so much. I hope she can forgive me for leaving her."

"It'll work out for the best. A little more time is hopefully all she needs."

Taking the weeds to the dustbin, I see Jordan. He's delivering a new pile of leaflets. Waving, I hurry inside to avoid talking to him. I wash my hands, using the nail brush to remove the stubborn dirt. The new material my sister bought is set on the table. The fabric with the colourful skateboards on catches my attention and I run my fingers over the print.

"I can make you a bag for uni if you'd like," Helen says as she appears from the pantry with a box of sewing pins.

"Where's Beatrice?" I ask, looking around.

"She's taking a call in the living room." Helen

takes a few pins out of the box and begins to tack the material.

"I would love a bag. Thank you."

Even if the skateboard pattern reminds me of Julian, I like it. One day, I'll welcome the bittersweet memory of the summer, but today, the wound is still too fresh.

"Why haven't you told Derrick you'll marry him?"

"What makes you so certain that my answer is yes?" she teases.

"He's living here, isn't he?"

She smiles. "I'll tell him yes, I'm just making sure he's sticking around first."

I hug her. "I'm happy for you."

"You'll be my maid of honour."

I nod, even though it wasn't a question. Everything is falling into place for me to leave for university without feeling as if I'm abandoning my family who need me.

Beatrice practically skips back into the room. Her smile beams brightly. "We have our first order. I'm going to personally deliver fifty overnight bags tomorrow morning."

My sister and I perform a high five as laughter fills the room.

"I need to pack my belongings. Please get the order together for me to collect later today," Beatrice instructs Helen as she clasps her hands together in satisfaction.

As I open the door to join Derrick in the garden, a pair of boots is hiding behind a huge bouquet of flowers.

"Does Kara Edwards live here?"

"Erm, thanks. That's me."

He gives me the wildflowers and I sit on the steps, staring at the sealed card. My name is neatly displayed on the envelope.

"Who sent the flowers?" Derrick asks, bringing me out of my trance.

I hold up the card. "I don't know."

He pats me on the back before disappearing into the house. I flip the card over in my fingers a few times before I open it.

Forgive me for not delivering this better. I'm sorry.

The message doesn't even tell me who they're from. There are only two people that owe me an apology, but the note doesn't clear up my confusion of who sent them. One thing changes though. Tonight, when I go to bed, I charge my phone.

CHAPTER THIRTY FOUR

BEAR

Skating up the small ramp, my caballerial flip takes flight. Flipping the board comes with ease, unlike my uneasy mind. My summer is spiralling out of control, and I can't get a grip on the way Kara made me feel. She gave me a new reason to stick around the park. Her energy gave me a refreshing view of the place. Now she's gone, the place just isn't the same. Even worse, I feel like Kara took a part of me too.

When I start university, there's a slim chance I might see her. We'll be in the same city, but the campus is big, and she won't be looking my way. Any chance of her liking me vanished when I stuck in the knife. Why did I listen to Toby? Having the summer with her would've been enough; it would've been better than losing her like this.

My lunch break ended twenty minutes ago. I

probably should get back, although Vinnie will have everything under control, even if he's cursing me for being irresponsible. When avoiding my problems, I usually find myself drawn to the skate park, and having one in my garden makes it easy to escape the world. I step off the skateboard, flip it into my hand, and place it against the wall. I remove my helmet and throw it into the shed. I slow my pace as I look out onto the lake, remembering my dumb decision. The one I can't forget. The route back to the theme park is filled with memories of Kara. A voice behind me brings me out of my slump.

"Where is she?" Toby shouts.

I don't turn around. This guy is already wasting my time and I don't want to have this conversation with him. "How should I know?" I bark out.

It's a lie. More than one person has told me Kara left with her suitcase, and I'm surprised Antony didn't tell Toby. I'm not going to make this easy for him though. If he's as close to her as he makes out, he'll figure it out.

"What did you do?"

I clench my fist and turn to face Toby. What did *I* do? More like what did he do? His red face simmers my emotions. Whatever he expected to happen didn't involve him being shut out by Kara.

"Look, I think you should calm down." I try to reason with him, although I want to punch him.

"Don't tell me what to do." The vein in his forehead pulses with every breath.

My arms swing wide as if I'm announcing my news to the world. "I broke up with her. Everything after that is on you."

Leaving is better than punching him, and my temper is almost at boiling point. Turning away from him, I storm away, pounding my feet into the floor with every step. I'm angry with him, but mostly, I'm angry with myself. Toby doesn't follow me, and I don't look back to see where he went.

Vinnie shakes his head as I approach the deck. I ignore him until my lifejacket is in place.

"If I were your boss, I'd fire you," Vinnie teases while looking up from the ground where he squats to fasten his shoelace.

"Lucky for me, you're not."

"Your mood swings are getting unbearable. You need to step out of this funk and stop feeling sorry for yourself. Go tell her you made a mistake."

"I can't. She isn't even here." I pull on my hair to relieve the tension in my scalp.

"There's no such word as can't."

"Maybe in theory there isn't. My dad would kill me if I took off again."

Besides, what if she doesn't want me? The pain in my chest would double.

"It's not like you're helping anyway. All you're doing

is stopping anyone from having fun. The last child you helped into the boat didn't even move after your talk on capsizing. You're like the anti-fun clown minus the makeup, although your face has always looked funny."

I glare at him, trying not to smile. "I could fire you for insubordinate behaviour." The corners of my lips waver slightly.

"We both know you can't function without me."

I grab hold of the rope to help bring a swan back into the dock. Vinnie fills the boat straight away with a waiting family.

"Was it busy while I was gone?"

"Every swan has been in use since the start of our shift. Your head is too far in the clouds for you to notice. If you aren't going after the girl, you need to get your head back in the game."

"What makes you such an expert?"

He holds his hands up in defence. "I'm not, but I'm also not an idiot. I could see the chemistry between the two of you." He shields his eyes to look across the deck. "Oh, boy. You're in trouble now."

My gaze follows Vinnie's to see an angry fairy godmother approaching us. Her sparkly pink feather boa blows wildly in the wind.

"So nice to see you, Lynne." I muster as much enthusiasm as I can.

"Don't play games with me. What's happening with Kara?" Her usual carefree attitude is missing from her voice.

"I don't want to talk about it, so respect my privacy. I screwed up. I don't need you to rub salt in the wound."

"Fix it." She gives me a stern look.

"I can't." I shake my arms in the air with frustration.

"He won't," Vinnie says as I glare at him.

"Why is everyone getting on my case?"

"Kara is the only girl you've ever shown any real interest in. Feelings like that aren't going to come around every day. Just look at your dad. He's never found anyone else after your mum. When are you going to wake up and see what was right in front of you?"

"This isn't a fairy-tale, there's no happy ending. My place is here, alone."

"Can I kick him now?" Vinnie jokes.

"Some friend you are."

"I could shake you," Lynne says.

"You're both ruining my pity party."

Heading into the control room, I close the door behind me, hoping they'll both disappear. Even this little room reminds me of Kara. I can't escape her memory anywhere. The flowers I sent yesterday were a stupid idea. Trying to avoid everyone isn't working and I haven't got a clue what to do now. Expect to keep my head down and hope everyone leaves me alone.

CHAPTER THIRTY FIVE

KARA

The material flies through the machine, heating the room. Beatrice leaving means I've been promoted to head assistant; a role I'm taking very seriously. I don't need any boys or theme parks messing with my head; sewing with my sister is the place I want to be. They say staying home is the new going out. The proof is in my new bag which is already waiting for me upstairs. Helen, queen of speed, made it before I woke up this morning, and she said I could make a purse with the offcuts of fabric.

Being her assistant also puts me in charge of breaks. Daydreaming comes with a price. It's already an hour after lunchtime. I shout to Derrick out of the window as the kettle boils. The table is full of Helen's equipment, so we take the sandwiches I made into the living room. Derrick kneels on the floor, trying not to dirty anything. There's a knock at the door and we all stare at one another blankly.

"I didn't order anything else," Helen says, as if we've caught her out. The attention shifts over to me when Helen decides the person is not for her.

"I got one bouquet of flowers, one time. It doesn't mean the person at the door is for me," I say, shaking my head.

"I'll get it," Derrick says, abandoning his sandwich. Helen and I both listen to every sound as he opens the door. Even holding my breath, the voices are too quiet. When he returns, he leans against the doorframe, trying to act causal.

"Helen, can I see you in the kitchen?" he asks in a light tone.

"I was just going to finish my sandwich," Helen says.

He gives her a look that means it wasn't a question. They quickly leave the room while my gaze stays pinned on the door. A sheepish-looking Toby appears with wild hair and sleepy eyes. I knew he would turn up eventually. I'm no longer angry with him. I've never been good at fighting with him, but it doesn't mean I forgive him.

"Hi, Toby," I say, curling my legs up onto the sofa while taking a bite of my sandwich. He shuffles his feet across the floor, sitting down next to me. He avoids eye contact, biting his lip. This is typical Toby behaviour when he's nervous.

"Can you forgive me for being a complete tool?" He plays with his feet, keeping his head down.

"You *were* a tool." I agree with him.

"I know. I'll beg if it'll help my case." He clasps his hands together.

"Did you send the flowers?"

He shakes his head. The large bouquet is in the hallway and there is no way he missed it.

"I wish I could take credit for them, especially if it gets me back in your good graces, but they're not from me."

Deep down, I knew they weren't from Toby. I know who sent them, but I wanted proof before I could accept the truth. Julian is sweet. He's a kind and caring person. My gut tells me he's the one who sent the flowers. The problem is, I have no idea what the flowers mean. Sorry I broke your heart? Sorry I made a mistake? A glimmer of hope is a dangerous thing when I have no idea what to do with it.

"Are you okay, Kara?"

"What?"

I'd tuned Toby out while I was thinking about Julian.

"I said what do I have to do to get you to forgive me?" he says.

"I'm not mad at you anymore. Don't get me wrong, you're not my favourite person right now. You ruined my adventure."

"I know and I'm sorry." He frowns.

"Are you admitting you did something wrong?" I watch his expression.

He scratches his cheek. "I should have trusted your judgement."

"Yes. I can handle myself. I don't need you to act like my big brother."

"I couldn't help it. I didn't want to lose you."

"We're like family. Nothing will change that." I have faith we can get through anything together even if one of us caused the problem.

"I was wrong to interfere." He looks repentant and I'm glad he knows he was wrong to interfere.

"You were. If I wanted your help I would ask, you shouldn't take my choices away from me. I need to stand on my own two feet and make my own mistakes. I'm over our fight, but I need a little time to clear my head and turn these past few weeks into a distant memory. I don't want another romance. From this day forward, I want friendships, and lots of them, but *I* want to choose them. No confusing messages or over-analysing feelings. Just fun, caring friends."

I'm not over it, but it's time I need. Toby's words are nice to hear. I'm glad he's sorry, but my feelings are still raw. Nothing he says is going to change that.

"My assumption about Bear missed the mark. He's not who I thought he was."

"What do you mean?"

"He told me he cared about you before I left."

I run my hand through my hair. I know Julian

cares about me. *That's* the frustrating part. I don't want to talk about this with Toby though, so I change the subject.

"You and I are two peas in a pod. I bet you didn't tell Sophie how you feel."

He clears his throat. "It's too late now. I'm pretty certain I won't be welcomed back to the theme park."

"What did you do?" I clasp my knees tightly together.

"I quit. It took me a while to realise you weren't coming back. It was like a lightbulb turning on. Halfway through my shift, I knew you weren't in the theme park. I threw down my zombie jacket, screamed like I was in pain, and stormed out of the haunted house."

I shake my head. "You screamed?"

"Like I was turning into a monster. I probably scared people half to death, but it felt good."

I swallow down my laughter. "Has anyone ever told you that you take things too far?"

"You'd have loved to join in."

"Maybe."

The corners of his lips drop into a frown. "When we start university, I'm leaving you in charge of all the important decisions. I cause too much trouble."

"You've got that right." I tease.

I'm taking control of who I make friends with, even if it's not who Toby would have wanted. My eyes are open now. I'm going to handle my own relationships and make sure Toby doesn't mess anything up for me.

"Let me make it up to you. I'll take you to see whatever girly movie you'd like. I'll even buy the popcorn and stay awake until the end."

"You're a charmer."

"I'll go one better and throw in some ice cream. How does that sound?"

"Actually, can I take a rain check? I'm feeling sleepy."

It's a half truth. I'm not in the mood to play nice anymore. I feel drained of energy and need to recharge. Unfortunately, Toby sees straight through me.

"And tomorrow night you're washing your hair?"

"That's not what I meant, I'm not avoiding you. I just need some space tonight."

"As long as we can be friends again?"

I give him a push and he lands face-down on the sofa cushions. It's hard to stay mad with Toby. He isn't perfect, but he tries to be good. In his own misguided way, he was looking out for me. Now we're both back to square one. No summertime plans or holiday romances. At least we have each other.

"Okay, if you want to see a movie, I can find a period drama, but I'm expecting pizza."

"I probably deserve the torture."

He ducks as I swing at him with a small, square pillow. Toby grabs a cushion, aiming it right at me. I get a few hits in before he wrestles me to the ground, ruffling my hair as I squeal.

"They've made up," Derrick shouts from the hall as he leaves the house.

Toby smiles at me. "I know it will take time for you to forgive me, but at least you like me again a little more, right?"

He does his best lost kitty impression. I use the moment of weakness to flip him off me.

"You know I can't stay cross with you. Now let me look for that perfect movie."

"That's my girl."

———

Two litres of ice cream, a box of popcorn, and a bottomless cup of Coke later, we're back on track. Toby gives me the remote control to turn off the rolling credits.

"*The Avengers* movie is one of my new favourites," Toby says.

I nod to agree. "I'm over full. No pizza for me tonight."

"You should've shared the Ben and Jerry's Phish Food ice cream."

Once I agreed to watch a movie with Toby, he went to the shop while I searched Netflix's database.

"Give a girl a break. I'm drowning my sorrows and it tastes too good to give away."

"At least I've not got you drunk. Your sister doesn't need any more reasons to want to murder me," he jokes.

"She doesn't hate you. She just thinks you're a bit of an idiot sometimes. At the moment, I have to agree."

"Great. It can't be good if your best friend still wants to burn you alive."

"That's a little extreme."

"Maybe just make me walk across hot coals. How about tomorrow I take you to our treehouse? The fond memories might win me some points."

"Your mum's cookies might help too."

"It's a deal."

Once Toby leaves, my attention fixes on the small table in the hall. Next to my vase of flowers is a green, spiky cactus. Half the plant pot has a sticky note over it telling me the gift needs to go to my room immediately. Peeling back the note, I can see why. It reads, "Sorry I was such a prick." The wording isn't Hayley and Anna friendly, but it puts a smile on my face.

CHAPTER THIRTY SIX

KARA

A rainbow fur tail tickles my nose as Toby pirouettes around the small space. Most people would find this image disturbing, but I'm used to him. When Toby commits, he gives more than anyone should. That's what makes him unique and my best friend.

"When I said fluffy unicorn, this isn't quite what I had in mind. Just stay away from my cactus because I don't want either of you getting hurt."

It took Toby until lunchtime to turn up today, and now I know why. He spent the morning looking for his costume and a life-size unicorn now stands in my bedroom. His outfit is like a shell suit from the eighties, only with extra padding. He's very huggable which is wrong in so many ways.

"I went with my mum's suggestion to go big or go

home. You can brush me if you'd like," he says, pointing a hoof at my hairbrush.

Laughter escapes my lips while I shake my head. In all my unicorn fantasies, this never came up. His plan to cheer me up and make me forgive him is working perfectly, but I'm not ready to tell him yet. He's such a goofball and the pictures will make good leverage.

"Where are my cookies?" I ask.

"I put them in the kitchen with your sister. This outfit isn't exactly practical."

He tries to pick up the hairbrush, proving his point. Watching him attempt to grip the handle is like watching a drunk trying to locate a light switch. Realisation washes over me. Helen might be eating my cookies. I race out the door and down the stairs without a second glance, even the crashing noise behind me doesn't stop me. Helen has already made the tea and is waving the treats at me with a mischievous look. Beatrice sits at the table, pinning the latest masterpiece together.

Toby bounces downstairs like a herd of baby elephants. His movements are making my sides hurt with laughter. He loses his balance, slipping on the rug, and falls onto his butt. My laughter turns into a howl; even Beatrice cracks a smile.

"You're enjoying this too much," I say in between laughs.

Helen and I laugh like hyenas when he tries to stand and ends up back on the floor.

"At least university won't be dull with you two on campus," Helen says.

"I might still lose my best friend." Toby pouts.

It's hard to take him seriously in this outfit. Plus, I have no idea what he's talking about.

"Don't worry, you're stuck with me." I offer him a hand and pull him to his feet. "I'm done with boys, there's nothing to worry about in that department anymore."

"Not even if the guy is Bear, or do you prefer to call him Julian?"

"Why are you being so cryptic? What are you talking about?" I finish my cookie and grab another, dunking it into my tea.

"We're not the only ones going to Lancaster University." He doesn't seem completely happy with this knowledge.

"It's a big place. Thousands of people will be studying there." I narrow my eyes, wondering where he's going with this.

"I'm talking about one person in particular."

He raises his eyebrow, waiting for the penny to drop. I know what he's hinting at, but I'm finding it hard to believe.

"Surely Julian would've said if that was true."

Beatrice shrugs, showing she doesn't have any inside information.

"My source is reliable," he says in his best detective voice.

"That explains the flowers, I guess. He probably wants to be on good terms."

"You keep telling yourself that," Toby says, rolling his eyes.

I'm not sure how I feel about Julian being so close in a few weeks. Lancaster is a big place, so avoiding him shouldn't be too hard. The idea of seeing him, but not being able to be with him, is like a punch to the gut. His intense eyes flash in my mind, brooding Julian is one of my favourite looks on him, but I'd rather it be seductive. The problem is it makes me want to kiss him even more. Urgh, I can't escape him.

"It's time for me to change out of this outfit and move onto stage two of my plan." Toby announces.

"There's more to this madness?"

I laugh, welcoming the distraction. He holds his hoof up, indicating for me to wait as he disappears upstairs. Resting against the counter, I finish the rest of my tea. Beatrice carries on with her work while Helen washes the cups.

"It's nice to see you again, Beatrice," I say.

She's started appearing in the kitchen like part of the family. She's becoming like a long-lost aunt rather than someone we met a couple of weeks ago.

"I'm afraid it's a flying visit. I've got another order to deliver of your sister's bags and then I have my own contract to fulfil."

"Are you making some fairy costumes?"

"Mermaids and waves are my new project. It's a secret though. Graham likes to make his own announcements."

"You're working with Julian's dad?"

"The order is for him, but I'll only drop it off. There are a few weeks of summer left. If you aren't full up on adventure, I'd love some help with my creations. Helen says you make a good assistant and I could use a hand."

"The offer is tempting, but I don't want to return to Blue Oaks."

"I live in a cottage by the sea. My corgi, Tiny, and I live alone. You'll be lucky to see another person the whole time you're there. My home is down a secluded road. Don't answer me yet. Take until tomorrow to think about it."

"Beatrice might have work for you while you're away at university. This could be a good opportunity for you," Helen pitches in.

Before I can get a word in Beatrice repeats her words. "Don't make a quick decision. Sleep on it."

I nod in response. Helen is right. It's a good opportunity and Beatrice is a generous lady, I should be jumping at the chance. My relationship with Toby is back on track, a couple of weeks away won't make much difference, but something is holding me back.

When Toby returns, he's holding two tickets to

see unicorns in the local farm. Ponies dressed up as mythical creatures is closer to what I had in mind. He waves the tickets at me and I accept them before dragging him out of the door.

CHAPTER THIRTY SEVEN

BEAR

Brushing my teeth is one of my favourite times of the day. It symbolises a fresh start or a new chapter. The minty flavour fills my mouth as I run the toothbrush back and forth. My mind clears of distant dreams. I'm ready to stop dwelling on the past.

I grab a banana for my breakfast from the fruit bowl. Hovering over my father's mug, I check his coffee level. He's sitting in his usual chair with his glasses resting on the end of his nose and his head in the newspapers.

"You need to go change your clothes," my dad says, thrusting his paper towards me.

"What. Why? What's wrong?" I ask with concern.

He's usually concentrating so much on his work, he hardly ever acknowledges my presence in the morning, never mind my clothing. Today, there's something different about him. Clearing his throat, he removes his glasses to take a closer look at me.

"I spoke to Beatrice yesterday and she filled me in on the Kara situation." He points the arm of his glasses at me as he speaks. His expression tells me he's all business, even as he talks about my personal life.

"I'm not following you. What does that have to do with my outfit? Kara's gone, my relationship with her is over. Your chance to recruit her for functions is not going to happen. I'm sorry I let you think securing a deal with Beatrice was all me."

I ramble under the pressure of his gaze. We never talk about relationships or our feelings. He studies me, watching my every move.

"Do you like this girl?"

"Yes, of course."

"Then what are you still doing here? Go get her."

"But..." I step towards him.

He waves his hand to silence me. "Only one woman ever gave me butterflies. She made me feel alive, and I would give a thousand lifetimes to have her back. If Beatrice's words hold even an ounce of truth, the two of you sound perfect for each other. No excuse is good enough to throw that away. It doesn't hurt that she's good for the park too. Now, go set this wrong on the right path. I look forward to meeting her."

I stare at him for a moment with my mouth hanging open. His stern glare tells me there's no room for arguing. All my excuses evaporate from my mind. He's telling me to go get what I want and I'm wasting time. There's nothing left to hold me back. I turn and run back upstairs. I quickly change into jeans and a white t-shirt before setting off down to the lake. I need to talk to Vinnie. I'm deserting him again, only this time, he won't mind.

"I'm going to see Kara," I say as I run down the deck.

"At last. What took you so long?"

The park doesn't open for another ten minutes. Instead of finishing the ride set up, he places the closed sign back on the entrance, dusting his hands off like the day is over.

"What are you doing?"

"I wouldn't miss this for the world. I'm coming with you."

"I don't need you to laugh at my rejection."

"There's no point arguing. 'm coming for moral support. There isn't a damn thing you can say to stop me. Besides, I can't run this ride by myself."

I don't point out he's lying. He's managed the swan ride plenty of times on his own. I don't need anyone to hold my hand but I know he's only trying to help.

"I'll find you some eye candy to work with."

"It hurts that you think I would change my mind so easily. Stop stalling, and let's go."

We don't make it far before Lynne is chasing us. I

roll my eyes when she lines up with us, matching our pace.

"Have you come to your senses?" She asks, breathless.

"Yes. I'm going to her house right now. I don't need either of you to assist me."

"Do I have time to change out of my fairy costume?"

I stop dead in my tracks. What did I do in a former life to warrant needing two people to hold my hand? There's no point in having the same argument again. After a deep breath, I slowly nod. I'm not trusted to stay put, so I end up with a fairy babysitter while Vinnie and Lynne change. Pacing up and down, I try to ignore everyone walking by. A few of the female staff offer me a thumbs up, but I try to block them out. Lynne must be telling everyone the situation rather than concentrating on getting her clothes on. I bang on the door, shouting for her to hurry up.

"Are you ready?" I bark out once they reappear.

Lynne smiles sweetly in response. Vinnie's lip curls, resembling an evil villain rather than a friendly smile.

My last gate crasher comes at the train platform. Sophie and I have never been friends, but she has a thing for Toby. I'm not surprised to see her.

"Please don't fire me," Sophie says, laughing nervously.

She has her fairy make-up on, jeans, and a black t-shirt. She looks like Harley Quinn, only with more glitter. Lynne waves a packet of baby wipes at her. Vinnie wolf whistles, admiring her figure, which earns him a stuck-out tongue.

"You should all lose your job," I say.

"Stop being so grumpy, or he'll never take your sorry ass back," Vinnie says.

"I'm so happy I brought you," I scowl.

Boarding the train, I head for first-class, hoping for a little peace. In reality, I end up paying for four tickets and a round of coffees. The upside being, I don't get a second to doubt my actions. It's full steam ahead.

When we arrived at Hexham train station, I used the address on Kara's file to arrange a taxi. Now, the small cottage she lives in stands before me. My cheer-leaders wait at the side of the road. Taking a deep breath, I open the gate and walk up to the door. I knock, trying not to make it sound like a tune. My palms feel clammy when I realise I don't have a clue what I'm going to say. I should have kept the cactus as an ice-breaker rather than sending it to her. Turning back to my friends, I see them trying to encourage me. Lynne crosses her fingers, holding them high in the air.

The door opens to reveal an older version of Kara. She has the same curls and button nose. She smiles, waiting for me to speak. I clear the frog in my throat before opening my mouth.

"Could I speak to Kara, please?" My voice is rough like sandpaper.

"I'm sorry. She isn't here."

I should have phoned ahead. That would've been the sensible option. My heart starts to sink as I take a single step back. My nerves turn to disappointment. I've made a mess of everything yet again.

"Thanks," I say before turning back to my friends.

"Wait," says the voice behind me. She holds her finger up in the air, waving it at me a few times before she speaks again. "Let me grab my coat and I'll take you to her."

CHAPTER THIRTY EIGHT

KARA

"That one looks like a bunny if you squint a little," I say, pointing to the big fluffy cloud moving across my vision. I put my arm back behind my head, staring up at the sky.

"If a five-year-old drew a rabbit then maybe you're right."

Toby grabs a grape out of the picnic basket before returning to my side on the blanket. The long grass hides us from view as we lazily enjoy the warm breeze. Toby is trying to remind me of all the reasons we're best friends, and this brings back good memories. We've spent many nights here, looking at universities and dreaming up adventures.

"See if you can do any better then."

He flicks my elbow with his finger. I turn to look

at him, about to tell him off when he interrupts me. "Can we be serious for a minute?"

"Sure. What's on your mind?"

"I want to say sorry for ruining your summer."

"You've already said sorry a hundred times."

He sits up, running his hands through his hair. "Sometimes I underestimate how lucky I am to have a best friend like you. This is me admitting I should look after you better."

"You're forgiven. You *are* lucky to have me. I can see how sorry you are, and I hope you won't do anything like this again. Let us shelve the whole disaster as done and dusted. No more talk of Julian, theme parks, or what could've been. I want to move on from the experience."

"Why didn't you go with Beatrice? It would've been an amazing opportunity."

"Being around her would only remind me of Julian. I want a break from thinking about summer love."

"You really like him, don't you?"

"We were never serious. Can we please forget about it now? Come on. Let's get out of here."

Slapping his knee, I use it to help myself up. He checks his phone, giving me a look I can't read, which is strange because I know all his usual expressions. He folds the blanket, glancing at me every two seconds like he's up to something.

"We've somewhere to be," Toby says hastily.

He leaves the basket and blanket, racing across the open meadow. I should've seen this coming with his shifty behaviour. Sprinting after him, I try to catch up, but he's too fast. He doesn't give me a second glance as he enters the forest. By the time I slow my pace at the treehouse, he's nowhere to be seen. No sounds from the woodland around me give away his location. I look up into the tree. My feet slot into the wood, finding their way to the top. I pull myself up onto the handmade treehouse. I have to take a second look at the person at the top. My breath catches in my throat.

"Julian."

Instead of answering me, he pulls me into his arms, placing a toe-curling kiss on my lips.

"Give me one date. No misconception about this not being what I want, I like you and I'm not letting you go without a fight."

My argument with Toby wanders through my mind. I'm a small-town girl. I don't have any money or a great love for charity. I'm not a walking legacy, I'm an ordinary girl. Just me, Kara Edwards. Plain and simple.

"How can someone like you want something serious with someone like me?" I look into his eyes, trying to read his handsome face.

He kisses the tip of my nose. "You underestimate yourself. Being around you makes me want to be myself. I know you've got no interest in my money or social status. You like me and I like you. We connect. It's that simple. You and I fit perfectly together."

He cups my face and rubs his thumb over my lower lip. The look in his eyes tells me he believes I can be the girl he wants me to be. Being with Julian comes easily. The qualities I thought mattered are not what Julian says he needs. My mum never made me feel like I was worth sticking around for and Toby's words still cut deep, but I want to believe Julian.

"You'll get sick of me."

"That's not going to happen. I can be more than a short fling, just give me a chance to prove myself. One date is all I'm asking to show you that you'll want more of me."

Julian's words make it sound like he would be the lucky one. His lips hover over mine, tempting me. A taste is all I need. He waits for my answer, which I whisper, right before he unleashes hot fury on my mouth.

"What do you have in mind?" I ask.

"Hold that thought. First, we should tell our audience you didn't shoot me down."

He gestures to the treehouse window. I lean over Julian's shoulder to peer down to the ground. His mint and cherry aroma has me licking my lips. Applause comes from my group of friends when they see us. These people came to see me. I didn't need Toby this summer. I made my own connections. I'm proud of the way I made friends. Lynne waves and I smile.

"What's everyone doing here?"

"I didn't want to miss a happy ending," Lynne shouts, a huge grin on her face.

"I thought we were friends. You didn't even say goodbye. Plus, I needed to make sure Bear got here safely. I'm sick of looking at his moody face and I'm here to make sure he didn't chicken out," Vinnie says, making me laugh.

"I'm just a stowaway," Sophie adds. Her arm rests on Toby's shoulders.

"We'll be right down," I say. I nip at Julian's lip one last time before climbing to the ground. "How long are you guys staying?"

"The theme park needs its dream team. Our adventure will be short lived," Vinnie says.

"What can I do to make your visit count?" I ask.

"Some home comforts would be good," Vinnie says.

"We've got some swans at the local park, although you can't ride them."

Vinnie laughs. "I was thinking of food and a comfy seat."

"I can offer a barbecue and a camping chair," I say, looking to Helen for approval. She nods.

"We need to be on the last train home. What about you, Bear?"

"I'm going to book a hotel for the night. I'll make sure the three of you are on the train."

"We don't have much space, but I can sleep on the sofa and you can have my room," I suggest.

Julian is about to argue when Helen gives him the look. The one that says there is no negotiation to be made. I try to suppress my smile.

Back at the house, Derrick helps the guys set up the seating area and lights the fire. Lynne, Helen, Sophie, and I prepare the food.

"I can't believe all of you are actually here," I say.

"The park didn't feel the same without you. Looking at Bear's gloomy face was too depressing," Lynne says, echoing what Vinnie had said.

"Kara's worn the same miserable expression. Who'd have known the summer club would've been so good for everyone?" Helen says.

"Wait, you already knew him before you came to the park?" Lynne asks.

"I'd only met him a handful of times. We weren't friends or anything."

"I heard he's a big shot skateboarder," Sophie adds.

"That's half right. He's won a few competitions, but it's the sports charities he loves," Lynne says.

"My girls were in his class earlier in the summer. He's a kind guy, helping people everywhere he goes," Helen says.

"I don't think he sees it like that," I say.

I've already filled Helen in on who Julian is. The girls were sceptical at first. They didn't want to believe he could be a mistake for me. Julian turning up today changes everything. He's he guy we thought he could be, and my heart is swoon ng.

After a tearful goodbye, my friends leave for the train station. Helen sets Julian ι p in my bedroom and I settle on the sofa for the night

CHAPTER
THIRTY NINE

KARA

"I hope you weren't expecting a posh restaurant and me in a suit," Julian says as he passes me a hotdog from the fast food van. The smell lingers in the air and my stomach rumbles.

Helping myself to the sauces, I smother the sausage in mustard and ketchup. "This is great."

I should try and eat this like a lady, which would be easier if I hadn't loaded it with so much sauce. Instead, I pretend this isn't a date, that he isn't looking at me, and I'm not trying to impress anyone. Julian smiles before he bites into his own food. He doesn't seem to notice I'm a little nervous, or my lack of manners.

"So, what do you want to go on first?" I ask.

"I think we should have a kissing session on the

Ferris wheel," he says with a sparkle of mischief in his voice.

A laugh escapes my lips, breaking the tension. He's here to be with me. I need to remember that. He doesn't care about the material things.

Throwing my dirty napkin in the bin, I place my arm around Julian's back. He rewards me with a kiss on the head. The fair comes to town a few times a year and we managed to catch it on the last day. It doesn't compare to Blue Oaks, however, it's marvellous for our first date. Julian buys tickets for the Ferris wheel. He offers the guy a little extra cash before he joins me on the seat. I pretend not to notice his gesture.

"The view from the top won't be as impressive as Blue Oaks cable cars, but we'll be able to see a glimpse of the river," I say.

"The view I want to see is inside this cart."

"You're cute," I say, nudging him with my knee.

The ride starts slowly, moving us up to the top.

"Sorry. That line was cheesy. I'm no sweet talker, but it's the truth."

"If you can win me a cuddly penguin toy on the hoops, I'll be putty in your hands."

"A challenge on a first date might scare a lesser man. Lucky for you, I'm an expert. I've had years of practice with the hoops and I could do it blindfolded."

"Your skills give you an advantage. I bet you make all the ladies swoon."

He laughs. "Blue Oaks is my anchor. It's both a curse and a blessing. I want more with you, but my home will always be at the theme park. If you've big dreams of travelling or living on the wild side, you should probably let me down now before it's too late."

"The truth is, I would love a place to call home. My sister doesn't have space for me, and my dad's house has never been somewhere to stay for long. I know it's too soon to think Blue Oaks could be my home, although a permanent address is something I crave."

He rewards me with a kiss. The ride stops at the highest point. His soft lips brush against mine while he strokes my hair. Julian is giving me a glimpse of a future with a true home. He's everything I ever wanted and more, and my heart flutters.

"Come back with me. You don't have to work in the park, you can do whatever you like. Just give us a chance."

"Are you attending Lancaster University this September?" I ask.

He smiles. "Sorry if you thought you were escaping me, but you'll find me in the business division."

"Why didn't you tell me?"

"It's not located on the main campus, so I won't be that close, but I should've told you."

He looks sincere. I rub my fingers over his lips before kissing him again.

Once we leave the Ferris wheel, we make our way across the field. Julian makes hoop tossing look easy, and the other guys playing look like amateurs. The rings find their target like they're following a piece of string. He gets all three hoops on the bottles first time.

The little girl next to me tugs on her daddy's arm. "That's how you do it," she says, pointing to Julian's rings.

She looks hopeful until her dad misses the next shot. Julian buys three more hoops and wins another teddy. The guy next to us pulls at his hair as his ring skims the top of a bottle and falls to the ground.

"We need to find a loving home for this second penguin," Julian says, pretending to look around.

The little girl jumps up and down, trying to get his attention. The look of gratitude on the man's face when Julian passes over the soft toy fills me with pride.

"Thanks," he says.

"Anytime," Julian replies.

"Is there anything you're not good at?" I ask him.

"Getting you to like me."

"I think you're doing well at that."

"Best date ever," he whispers, right before he kisses me again.

My foot flips up, just like in the movies. I have to

agree, this has been perfect. Julian buys us candyfloss, and we take a slow, romantic walk home to finish the night.

———

Sleeping on the sofa isn't the most comfortable. The second there's movement in the house, I'm on full alert. The creak of the stairs interrupts my pleasant dreams. Rising from my makeshift bed, I push the blankets onto the floor, stretching my arms above my head. The crick in my neck is worth it to have everyone I care about under one roof. The click of the front door has me curious to see who's awake.

Once in the hall, I find my latest present from Julian; a pink skateboard with red wheels. I bite my lip to lessen the smile. There's a card which reads, "I wish I could have you in my world. A gift so you can remember me."

His suggestion for me to leave with him took me by surprise, and I didn't want to make a quick decision whilst drunk on lust. Taking a chance on love is a scary thought. I know Julian cares about me, but Helen's the only person I've ever relied on. Making myself vulnerable is something I try to avoid. I want to be with Julian, but what if it doesn't work out?

Doubt sets in my mind. Maybe Julian thinks I didn't want to leave with him. Could the gift be a way of saying goodbye? Putting my slippers on, I step outside.

Julian's on a video call with Vinnie. Both have matching bed head and I instantly feel like I've intruded on their conversation.

"I'm so sorry," I say, cringing.

Vinnie pulls his duvet up over his chest. My eyes widen when I realise he's probably half naked and I wasn't supposed to see him like this. Vinnie laughs and Julian turns to face me.

"What's wrong?" Julian says. He doesn't seem to notice mine and Vinnie's moment.

"Your girlfriend has come to her senses and has seen I'm the better choice," Vinnie jokes.

"Did you just flash my girl?" Julian says, raising an eyebrow.

"How would I know she was going to creep up on you?"

"I didn't sneak up. After I saw Julian's gift, I thought he'd left."

"I'm not going anywhere until you tell me to," Julian whispers.

"It's too early for all this sweet talk," Vinnie says, covering his face.

"You're just jealous."

"I won't deny it." He pulls the covers up around his neck.

"Vinnie lost the girl of his dreams. That's why he's

so bitter." Julian appears to be challenging Vinnie to deny his accusation.

"This isn't about me. Now let me sleep."

He waves and ends the call.

I've never seen Vinnie with a girl. He's all flirt without the backup of a date. Maybe one day I'll get his story. After a few kisses with Julian, I leave him sitting on the step. Heading inside, I make myself a drink, settling on the sofa and welcoming extra sleep. Knowing Julian will be here when I wake makes my dreams even sweeter.

CHAPTER FORTY

BEAR

Kara is hot on a skateboard, and she drives me crazy every time she bites her lip. I'm struggling to keep my hands off her, especially when her cute curls flop in front of her face. She doesn't shy away from the tasks I set her, which is the only thing stopping me from kissing her. She's actually pretty good for a beginner.

"When can I get rid of the shin pads?" Kara asks optimistically.

"Whenever you want to graze your knee," I joke.

"Hey, who says I'm going to fall over?"

She wobbles a little before regaining her balance. Kara looks smug until she realises the skateboard isn't going to stop. Her slow decline begins to speed up. The hill is only small, although it's enough to send her falling into my arms. Kara's beautiful eyes lock with mine as her cheeks glow with a pink tinge.

"Did I ever tell you how pretty you are?" I ask.

"You're a bit yummy too."

"And you haven't even seen me naked yet."

The shade of her cheeks deepens into a dark red glow. She's cute when she's flustered. Kara buries her head into my chest, hiding her face.

"We don't have to rush into anything. I'm only teasing you," I say. I stroke my hand down the side of her arm and take hold of her hand.

"You know how to make a girl blush." She interlocks her fingers with mine.

"I can't help it when it gets you where I want you." A smile spreads across my face.

"And where is that?"

"You snuggled into my chest." I pull her in close.

"You're sweet like a sugar doughnut. No fancy sprinkles needed."

I laugh. Kara's words carry some truth. We don't need to have fancy dates or over the top gestures. We work because of the simple things.

"You're beautiful just the way you are too." I kiss her lightly on the lips.

"I'm not poetic. What I'm trying to say is you make me feel like nobody has before."

I kiss her again. "You should give me a chance to show you how good I can be." I want a real chance with her.

"What do you think I'm doing?"

"Be mine, Kara. Let's make it official. I want you

to be my girlfriend. I'm playing for keeps, not for short term hot kisses, although those are good too." I play with the soft curls of her hair, teasing it between my fingers.

"I'm already yours, Julian," she whispers.

They're the only words I need to hear. Kara makes me want things I never thought I'd be able to have. She's funny, sweet, beautiful, and kind. I see her as my equal, not just someone pretty on my arm. Gently, I give her another chaste kiss on the lips, knowing we're not alone in the park.

"Come on. Let's take this to the street before we get in trouble."

"I can't imagine you being in trouble with anyone."

"Wait until you get to know my dad."

I can already see him liking Kara. That doesn't mean he'll go easy on me in front of her, but I think she can handle herself.

"Why? Are you always late doing your home-work?" She playfully pinches my bicep.

"You wish. I'll finish my coursework early if it means I get to see you quicker."

"You're sweet and too perfect. I'm waiting to find your flaw, if only to make myself feel better."

I laugh. Kara has seen my blemishes and easily overlooks them. I'm not perfect, but I want to be for her. She only sees the good in me and it warms my heart.

"I don't do my own laundry."

It's a lame attempt at giving her a small win, but she's straight onto me.

"There must be a bigger demon in your closet. Come on, spill your darkest secrets."

"I aspire to be one of the seven dwarfs. The one they call Grumpy."

She laughs. "That I know. Keep going. I want the juicy stuff."

I flip my hair over. "Wanting to impress a girl is new for me. You're the first one." I look into her eyes, hoping she can hear the sincerity in my voice.

When we reach the road, I take my skateboard out of its bag. I lead the way down the small hill with Kara following slowly.

"I bet you were popular with the girls in school."

"I went to an all-boys grammar school. My dad didn't want me getting distracted. I've dated a few girls, don't get me wrong, but mostly ones who cared more about social status."

"Oh, I care about those things too."

I laugh. "So that's why you want to date me."

"No. That's why I'm going to beat you home. I need social status bragging rights."

She picks up the skateboard, making a run for it. I closely follow, not even trying to steal the victory. She dances on the front step before going inside. After making drinks, she disappears upstairs to help Helen with something.

Hayley and Anna find me once I'm alone in the

living room. Sitting on the sofa, I sip the coffee. Hayley sits on my right and Anna on my left. They both cross their legs, staring at me intensely.

"Kara said she wouldn't bring a boy home unless he was special. You invited yourself. Does that count?" Hayley says.

I laugh and almost spill my drink. Who would've known these two sweet girls would be the ones to give me a grilling?

"She's an extraordinary girl."

"Lynne told us you're the Blue Oaks prince. Does that mean Kara will be a princess?" Anna pitches in.

"I think Lynne watches too many fairy-tale movies."

"Should we call you Julian or Bear? Even my mum says she isn't sure," Hayley says.

"Whatever you'd like to call me is fine."

"But not a prince?" Anna asks.

A laugh tickles my throat as I shake my head. Lynne was only here for less than a day and she's already told them too much. I don't want that name to stick. It's bad enough when people figure out why they call me Bear.

"He can have the stamp of approval, don't you think, Anna?"

They talk like I'm not in the room. Unspoken words pass between them while I try not to feel the pressure.

"I'm glad to hear it," I say with a smile.

"If you hurt her, we'll break your nose," Anna says with a stern look, pointing her finger at me. Satisfaction is written all over their faces as they leave me to my coffee. Toby lingers in the doorway and I wonder how long he's been standing there.

"What they said about breaking stuff applies to me too," Toby says in a joking way but I'm guessing he's being serious.

"Excellent."

There's a moment of tension between us as we stare each other down.

"We didn't get off to the best start and I'm sorry. If Kara likes you, that's good enough for me. I'm hoping eventually we can be friends."

"I'd like that."

I mean it too. Toby is Kara's best friend. Making an effort with him can benefit us both. I don't want anything to come between Kara and me again, I'm planning on sticking around. Being friends with Toby will make both our lives easier.

"Great." He taps the door frame with his thumbs.

"Great."

Now our manly chat is over, he gives a swift head nod and leaves me. I relax back against the sofa. I sip my coffee, hoping nobody else comes to grill me on my intentions. Kara may not have a good relationship with her father, but the rest of them make up for it when it comes to the *dating my daughter* talk.

In my wildest dreams, I never imagined a big

family. There's something about this one I could fall in love with. Looking at the picture on the wall of Kara and her family, I can almost see myself in the background. As scary as it seems, I'm falling for this beautiful girl.

CHAPTER FORTY ONE

KARA

Resting my feet on Julian's knee, I take a handful of popcorn from the bowl. We've dimmed the lights and *The Notebook* is playing quietly in the background.

"This is how I would describe my ideal date," I say, putting a few pieces of popcorn into my mouth.

"What do you mean?"

"I'm talking about the low-key date night. Don't get me wrong, I have no objection to you trying to impress me, however, I'm a no fuss kind of girl."

"Shall I take the penguin back?"

I playfully throw a piece of popcorn at Julian's chest. "Don't you dare. Mr Blue is my favourite gift."

Julian laughs. "I thought he was purple." He takes the piece of popcorn and throws it into his mouth.

"He's a misunderstood shade of blue. The name is

perfect for him. If the theme park is looking for a new mascot, I could nominate him."

"Are you trying to demote me to plain old Julian?" He fakes a pout.

"No. I like keeping your name to myself." My words earn me a smile.

"The twins are thinking about calling me by my real name too."

"Hayley and Anna have good taste."

"I can't argue with that."

Julian's phone rings and he presses the red button.

"Who was that?"

He looks at his locked screen. "My dad."

I rub his arm. "Do you need to get back to the theme park?"

"Yes, but I don't want to leave you."

My heart flutters. I don't want to be apart from him either.

"I'm coming with you." I tell him.

"Are you sure?"

I knew his stay would be short term, but I want more time with him. Julian keeps his expression blank, giving no clue to what he's thinking, but my mind is made up. The idea of spending any time without him isn't an option. He's becoming the person I want to do everything with.

"Yes."

He kisses the back of my hand. "Okay then. I've

been monitoring the times and there's a train at ten in the morning."

"I think we should catch it. My mind's made up. Let's return to Blue Oaks together."

We settle into the movie while Julian strokes the top of my knee. Every so often, he glances at me when he thinks I'm not looking. Sometime before the end of the movie, I fall asleep, waking only to pull the blanket closer to my chest.

———

Someone's awake before seven. With a groan, I lock my phone after checking the time and rub the sleep from my eyes. The pottery clanks as the early riser starts making breakfast and the smell of toast has my stomach rumbling. Making my way into the kitchen, I find Helen. Pancakes, eggs, and juice make their way onto the table.

"Morning," Helen says.

I grumble a greeting. "It's too early and I need to pack."

My eyes widen and I cover my mouth, I look at Helen with shock. I forgot to tell her about my decision.

"I know you're leaving," she says, unsurprised.

"Sorry. We only decided last night. I should've told you, but I didn't want to disturb you."

"Julian travelled all this way to come and get you. It would be disappointing if you didn't go back with him. I love having you here, but I'll be glad to get my house back."

She hugs me tightly before going back to the cooker.

The twins bounce down the stairs. Anna takes a few crumpets out of the bread bin, placing them in the toaster.

Hayley shouts from the bottom of the stairs, "Breakfast is ready, guys."

"You'll wake the whole street and then I'll have to feed an even bigger army. Keep your voice down," Helen scolds.

Hayley rolls her eyes in response, making me smile.

The stairs creak as Julian and Derrick find their way into the kitchen. Julian wraps his arms around me and kisses me lightly on the cheek.

"Do we qualify for free theme park tickets now you're dating Kara?" Hayley asks.

Helen waves her spatula in the air, however, Julian beats her to answer.

"My favourite twins can have annual passes."

"Yes," they say in unison, pumping the air with victory fists.

Toby arrives as everyone takes their seat at the table. He leans against the kitchen counter.

"Are there any fire-breathing sausages today?" Toby says, rubbing his hands together.

Helen laughs. "Apple is the special ingredient in this batch. I'll try for the dragon ones next time."

"Kara is leaving, but that doesn't mean I can't call in for breakfast. You should stock them up. I'm going to help Derrick finish the garden."

"Let's hope Toby lasts longer than the rest of you," Derrick jokes.

"Wait, you're not coming back with us?"

Toby isn't good with conflict and probably doesn't want to face Antony. At the beginning of the summer, I'd have been nervous without Toby. Now, I'm not so worried.

"No can do. It's only a few weeks until I join you at university and I have things to do here."

That's probably a cover story for his real reasons, but I let it slide. He doesn't want to come back to the theme park and that's okay. I have Julian, Vinnie, and Lynne.

"Who's going to be my sleeping buddy?"

Toby raises his eyebrow, making me blush.

"Keep it PG," Helen says, looking sternly at Toby.

"You can stay with me. I'm sure I can find you a little space somewhere," Julian says.

The heat rises further up my face. I'm not used to being the centre of attention, never mind the innuendo.

After our food, I re-pack my suitcase. Catching the train is nothing like my last two experiences. I have a seat in first class, my boyfriend holding my hand, and a warm drink set out in front of me.

CHAPTER
FORTY TWO

KARA

Butterflies flutter in my stomach when I think about living with Julian. It's only for a few weeks, but it feels like a big deal. He kisses my lips, pushing me up against his front door. His hands run over my back until he firmly grabs my hips. He pulls me against his body as I wrap my legs around his waist. He blindly feels for the handle, allowing the door to swing wide open. Both of us and our luggage fall through. My hands run wildly over his hair as he caresses the soft skin on my stomach.

A loud cough startles us, interrupting our heated moment. Julian kisses my forehead before we break apart. He can't hide his surprise when he sees who it is. My lust and embarrassment drop away when Julian's body tenses.

"Beatrice, what are you doing here? Where's my dad?" His voice is laced with worry.

Beatrice's hand covers her mouth before she plasters on a fake smile. She's no actress. Her body is too rigid and it's obvious something is wrong.

"Now, before you go crazy, your father's fine. There's nothing to worry about. I'm here to pick up a few things to take to the hospital."

"What do you mean there's nothing wrong? Why is he in the hospital? Why didn't anybody call me?"

Julian squeezes my hand tightly. His brow creases with concern. I put my hand on his lower back, offering a weak smile.

"The doctor says it's just a kidney infection and he'll be back on his feet in no time. They're keeping him in as a precaution, that's all."

He's quiet for a moment.

"I need to see him."

"He wants his day planner, but I can't find it and his secretary isn't answering the phone."

"I'm guessing the doctors want him to rest. I'll take care of his appointments. I don't want him doing anything stressful, so anything you've got in that bag which relates to work, take it out now." His tone leaves no room for argument.

Beatrice's nods and empties a few items from her bag. She leads us to her car, and we set off to the hospital.

When we arrive, I sit with Beatrice, waiting for

news from Julian. He was quiet on the drive in. Other than saying he wanted to see his dad on his own, he didn't say a word.

I tap my foot while chewing on my thumbnail.

"It's going to be okay," Beatrice says, rubbing my arm. She gets up from the chair. "I'm going to get us some drinks."

She disappears down the corridor. The visitors' waiting room is empty and my gaze wanders over the health posters. The small television in the corner is forecasting the weather, but I can't take it in. My mind feels scrambled. I'm worried about Julian and his dad and I wish there was something I could do to help. If Helen was the one in hospital, I'd be a wreck. His dad is his closest loved one. I want to make everything better, even though I can't. I continue to bite my nail until Beatrice returns a few minutes later. She passes me a hot drink with a biscuit on the top, giving my hands something else to do.

"I feel helpless," I say.

"Being here is the only thing we can do. Julian doesn't have any other family, and it'll be good for him to have someone to go home with."

"You care about them, don't you?" I ask her softly.

"They're both special people. Graham is a good friend. There was a time I hoped we'd be more, but he's made it clear he'll always be in love with his late wife." She doesn't seem sad, instead like she's reflecting on a memory.

"I'm sorry."

"Don't be. I've got a good life with a loving family and friends."

She places her hand on mine, giving it a little squeeze. Julian appears in the doorway and we both stand to wait for him to speak.

"My father would like to see you," he says to me.

Sucking in a deep breath, I smooth down my t-shirt, stepping towards Julian.

"There's no need to be nervous. He'll love you."

"How's he feeling?"

"He's taking antibiotics while they run a few more tests. The nurse says he'll be back to his old self in no time."

Julian's dad has a private room which is full of vibrant flowers. Even in the hospital bed, it's striking how much he looks like an older version of Julian.

"Dad, this is Kara, my girlfriend."

"It's nice to meet you, Mr. Oaks."

"We've already met briefly on the lakeside, I never forget a face. The pleasure is all mine. Beatrice speaks very highly of you. Please, call me Graham."

I tuck my hair behind my ear. "I hope all the things you've heard have been good."

"To win over Beatrice and my son, you must be special."

"I don't know about that." My cheeks warm with embarrassment of the attention.

"Do you read?"

"Dad!"

He points to the newspaper which I open, finding my way to the sports section. Shaking his head, he moves me to the first page.

"I like listening to a female voice."

Julian has a murderous gaze which he aims in his father's direction. I ignore him, reading from the beginning. He tells me when to skip and I work my way through the paper. Beatrice appears in the doorway to save me from the sports section. My dad only ever read the back of the newspaper and would never ask for my input. Instead, he'd ignore me. Even in this short time I've spent with Graham, I know he's a better dad than mine ever could be. He loves his son, even if he finds it hard to show it. My dad always makes me feel like a burden rather than someone he wants to share things with.

"How's everyone doing in here?" Beatrice asks.

"You're right. He's feeling a lot better," Julian says.

"I see he got you to read the newspaper," Beatrice says to me, laughing softly.

"I don't mind. It's good practice for when classes start."

"What are you planning to study?" Graham asks, genuinely interested.

"Unfortunately, I don't have a destiny like Julian. I'm doing my degree in media studies."

"What are you hoping to get out if it?"

"I'm leaning towards a career in journalism,

though I want to keep my options open. I'll be honest, I chose something I thought I'd enjoy rather than having a game plan."

"What about changing to business studies?"

"Dad! Kara, don't answer that. Let's get out of here before it's too late. We'll see you in the morning."

Julian pulls me out of the door as I offer a small wave. "I'm sorry about that," he says.

"I like your dad."

"He thinks everyone should follow his vision. The sooner you learn to be firm with him, the better."

"Does Beatrice keep him in his place?"

"More than he realises."

He uses his phone to call a taxi. Leaving Beatrice with Julian's dad, we go home. Julian stares out of the window on the way back to the house. He's quiet and hardly speaks a word. I rest my hand on his knee, hoping it's a small comfort for him. He doesn't brush me off, although he doesn't acknowledge me either. As soon as we step in the front door, Julian heads to his father's study. I wish he'd open up to me, but I don't want to push him further away. He dives straight into the paperwork on the desk. I make omelettes in the kitchen and take one to Julian. If reminding him he needs to eat is the only thing I can do, at least I've done my part.

"Thanks." He doesn't look up from the desk.

I chew on my lip for a few minutes, hovering over him. "Can I do anything to help?"

He looks up at me. "Sorry. Today was tough and scared me. My dad has always been strong, and seeing him lying there in a hospital bed was hard for me. He's always telling me how much the theme park needs me. I just never realised what he meant. I've got to get on top of the paperwork. There's nothing you can do," he says dismissively.

He kisses me on the cheek. I want to tell him everything will be okay. I want to ease his pain, but I can't find the words. I watch him work for a few more minutes before disappearing into the hall. The house seems bigger when I'm alone. Instead of worrying about the events of the day, I make plans to go out with Lynne.

CHAPTER
FORTY THREE

BEAR

My dad should be home in a few days. The nurses say he's doing really well and I'm trying to keep on top of his workload, but my dad's like a machine. He works all day, and sometimes through the night. Instead of standing in for his appointments, I cancel them. Even when he gets home, he'll need to rest. For the first time, I'll be in control and the one giving the orders, which I'm confident is the right thing to do. I knew the day would come but didn't realise it would be so soon.

The idea of losing him scares me and I never want to feel like this again. He's the only family I have, and I need him. The park needs him too. Putting my responsibilities on hold is no longer an option. I need to concentrate on what's important. Time isn't something I should take for granted. When the park needs me, I want to be ready. I can't fail my legacy. Blue Oaks is now my main focus and I want to take my role seriously.

My eyes flicker to Kara when I see her thin camisole top and tiny shorts. She puts a tray with toast and coffee onto the desk. We've hardly spoken since returning home from the hospital. Somehow, she knew I wasn't ready to talk, and I'm grateful for the time she gave me.

"Did you have fun last night?" I ask.

I saw her leave the house and return late. It's almost noon and she has messy bed hair. The toast smells delicious. It's easy to forget to eat when there's so much going on. I take a large bite, sinking my teeth into the marmalade.

"Sorry. You know how it is when girls get chatting. I went to see Lynne. She has the cutest dog ever."

"I'm glad you found a way to entertain yourself. The park has to come first which, sadly, means I'm going to be in this room more than I'd like."

"Business comes first. I understand."

I appreciate Kara caring about my life and the theme park. "Thank you."

My focus moves away from the beautiful curves of her body and back to the paperwork. Kara sits on the edge of the desk, allowing the shorts to creep higher up her legs.

"You misunderstood me," Kara says.

My gaze moves to her face. Her words completely

take me by surprise. "Blue Oak comes first, but that doesn't mean you can shut me out. The only reason I'm here is for you. Don't make me regret it. Find me something to do, even if it's highlighting keywords or filling in tick boxes."

I study her serious face which leaves no room for argument. This side of Kara drives me wild. Abandoning the paperwork, I step in front of her. She wraps her legs around me and I kiss her fiercely.

"You can help, but first, this outfit has to go."

I touch the strap of her top, but don't allow my eyes to drift any lower than her lips.

"Yes, boss."

She hops off the desk and I watch her leave the room. My mindset is all wrong. Keeping people at arm's length is a mistake and I don't want to push Kara away. My dad's illness is a sign, but I misunderstood the message. I need to keep the people I love close.

———

Kara spends her evening with Lynne, and I visit my dad. When I arrive, Beatrice is asleep in the chair next to the bed. The sound of me opening the door startles her. She quickly sits up. The lack of sleep is plain to see on her face.

"I'm going to go get some fresh air," she says, patting me on the back. Her bloodshot eyes tell me she needs more than a few minutes' break. The door clicks behind her and I take a seat in the visitor's chair.

"She's a good friend," my dad says, gazing at the doorway.

"Until you push her away again."

My words come out before I can help myself.

"Now you've got a girlfriend, you think you're some kind of expert?" he asks.

"No. It's just clear she would do anything for you. You're lucky to have her. She's kind, caring, and beautiful for an older woman."

"Don't let her hear you say that last part. My relationship with Beatrice is complex and not up for discussion. Did you reschedule my meetings for next week?"

"The nurses say you need to rest. There are no appointments in the book for a few weeks."

"Cancelling my meetings is a bold move."

"I chose a plot position for the water feature too."

He points at me, ready to argue. His lip twitches before he nods. "Okay."

I raise an eyebrow, waiting for his next move. He picks up the crossword puzzle and passes it to me.

"Eight letters, offer of marriage," I say, picking up from where he left off.

"Are you kidding me?"

"No. That's what it says right here. Five down, offer of marriage?"

He lets out a huff. "The answer is proposal. That's why Beatrice gave up on this puzzle. I can't wait to get out of this bed." He huffs in frustration.

"Once you're given the all clear, I'll happily take you home."

"How's the lovely Kara?"

"She's good, I think."

"I hope you're not messing it up."

"So, your love life is off-limits but mine's open season?"

"I like her, and I hope she's going to stick around. If we can't talk about business or women, what else is there?"

I think about his question for a second, hoping for a fast subject change. My dad bursts out laughing. It's a deep, uncontrollable sound. I haven't heard him laugh in years. The smile on my face is instant. We don't usually talk like this.

"Kara put me in my place this morning, telling me I shouldn't shut her out."

"And?"

"She's helping me with your office work."

"See, I knew there was something about her. Kara's going to be good for our family."

"Don't be jumping ahead. It's only early days."

"The moment she came to this town, I knew something had shifted in the air. I can see the change in you. My feelings for your mother were the same."

I want to tell him he's imagining things. It's on the

tip of my tongue, but the truth is, I think he's right. Kara set off a spark inside me. Confirming this won't do me any good, so instead, I read him the next crossword clue. Once he's out of the hospital, I'm going to make more time for us. The idea of losing him has shaken me up in more ways than one.

CHAPTER FORTY FOUR

KARA

It's late when I get back to Julian's house. My phone lost charge and I was having too much fun to realise the time. I silently creep towards the office, but find it empty. The desk light is on, but the room is vacant. I turn the switch off, which plunges me into darkness. After checking the kitchen, I presume Julian's gone to bed. I make my way up the stairs. A shadow moving across the landing quickens my pulse.

"You're home. I'm about to turn in for the night," Julian says.

I grip my chest with my hand. "You made me jump out of my skin. Has anyone ever told you this house is a little creepy at night. Don't get me wrong, it's beautiful, but there could be a family of six hiding in the basement and nobody would even know."

"Sorry for scaring you. It has security cameras. Trust me, you're safe here."

"How's your dad feeling?"

"He should be out in a day or two. He's driving the staff insane with his puzzles and constant muttering about the theme park. I think he's doing it on purpose so they let him leave earlier." Julian gives me a soft kiss on the lips before turning to enter his room.

"Night, beautiful."

"Julian."

He stops and turns to face me. It's too dark for me to see his expression. I close my eyes and take a deep breath. "Would it be okay if I slept with you tonight?"

"Of course you can. Come through when you're ready."

Tonight feels completely different from staying with Toby or taking shelter from the storm. I brush through my hair and choose a pair of pyjamas. They have a princess design, and they're figure-hugging, but not too revealing. I wouldn't know how to look appealing to a guy, but Julian never makes me feel anything less than perfect. Butterflies flutter in my stomach. Why am I so nervous? This is Julian.

I tiptoe through the hall, knocking before entering his room. He's lying on the bed, wearing a black t-shirt and boxers. I take a few seconds to admire his beautiful body. My face heats up when I realise he's watching me. He reaches out to me and I make my way towards him. I lift the duvet and snuggle in, burying my head into his chest.

"You're shaking. Relax, it's only me. I have no expectations of what's going to happen between us. I'm just happy to have you here."

Warmth fills my heart which calms my nerves. "You always know the right thing to say."

"We have all the time in the world. There's no need to rush into anything."

Looking into his eyes, I see the sincerity of his words. He softly strokes my hair, soothing my nerves. My fingers run down the length of his arm and onto his torso. His body is beautiful, even with clothes on. For tonight, this is enough. The thought of keeping Julian forever sweetens my dreams.

Just as I'm on the verge of falling asleep, I hear him whisper, "I love you."

When I open my eyes, he's already asleep. He looks peaceful. His long eyelashes flutter to a steady rhythm. My lips graze his soft skin and I can't believe how lucky I am to find someone so beautiful, inside and out. I watch him breathing until I fall asleep.

———

The next day, I leave Julian to his work and visit Lynne at the fairy castle. I queue with the children, ready to experience the magic. Once inside, the main door closes behind us. There is a glass statue in the centre of a fountain. Glitter sparkles from every surface. The blue glow of lights and soft music add to the magic. Little girls with wands run around the room, full of excitement. They look inside the trinket boxes, storybooks, and potion bottles at every turn. I watch their curious faces. This place is what fairy-tales are made from. I never came anywhere like this as a child and I think I missed out.

A spotlight falls on Lynne as her fairy godmother costume sparkles in the light. Her hands move with perfect elegance as she turns to face us.

"Children, I need your help to save Prince Charming. Can you help me find the special ingredients for the spell?"

Her performance is inspiring. The children disappear into the next room to continue their quest. I stay behind to talk to Lynne.

"Being the fairy godmother is your calling."

She laughs with the same light-hearted voice she uses to say her lines. "Blue Oaks is my home. I've been here since I was eighteen and I'll be here for years to come."

"I know what you mean. There's something about this place that captures your heart."

"In your case, I think you mean someone. I'll be making a request for you to join me for the winter nativity."

"Who would've thought Blue Oaks would feel like home? I want to try everything, experience every little detail of the whole park. I'll pencil the castle in for winter."

"I hope the castle becomes your favourite place. It'll be nice to have another permanent fixture around here. Some of us are in the park for the long haul, but my fairies always seem to move on to better things." There's sadness to her voice, like she wishes some of them would stay.

"Isn't it drama students that usually want to work with you?"

"Yes, then they leave me to work on cruise ships or return to theatre school."

"Does your crystal ball predict I'll stay here with you?"

"I have no magical powers, but I know when love is in the air." She holds her hands to her chest.

"Maybe I can find you a prince charming?"

"Don't you dare think of meddling in my love life."

I suppress a smile. "I'll try."

"If I wanted to date, I'd join a dating agency."

"Okay," I say with a beaming smile.

Before she can say any more, the red light on the wall turns on. It's the warning signal that another group of people are waiting to hear the story. She quickly takes her place as they begin to enter the room. I join the audience through the rest of the adventure, leaving Lynne to her work.

Once outside, I make my way over to the swan boats. Vinnie has two blonde, female co-workers with him. He waves when he sees me. I salute him and wave back. The girls are hanging onto his every word, so I leave him to it and make my way back to the house. A sense of belonging fills my heart. Blue Oaks theme park is beginning to feel a lot like home.

CHAPTER
FORTY FIVE

KARA

Pink rose petals decorate the hall. I follow them by candlelight into the kitchen. The smell of Italy has my mouth watering. Julian is singing along with the radio as I draw closer. His deep, husky voice fits perfectly with the song. I should've guessed he'd like Sam Smith. Roses and candles fill the room. It's sweet and fun, just like Julian.

I place my arms around his waist and kiss him on the cheek. "What's all this for?"

He turns to face me with a spoon in his hand and an apron around his waist. "This is my spin on your perfect date. A quiet night in with a movie and a home-cooked meal."

"I could get used to this."

"Lucky for you, I intend to keep you around."

"The pleasure is all mine. Let's hope your cooking is as good as your talking."

He gently bites my bottom lip and I grab hold of his t-shirt, fiercely kissing him. He peppers kisses along my cheek and onto my neck. He groans against my ear, making me melt further into his embrace.

When he returns to the stove, I take a seat at the table and watch him work his way around the kitchen. He spoons the pasta, meatballs, and sauce into two dishes and adds some herbs. Once he's finished, he places a delicious-looking dish in front of me. The second the sauce touches my taste buds, I'm in heaven.

"You put my omelette to shame. Why didn't you tell me you can cook?"

"I can't give away all my secrets at once. I don't want you to get bored of me."

"Fat chance of that. You're addictive."

He almost chokes on his pasta. Covering his mouth, he coughs a few times before clearing his throat. He takes a large drink of his water while I continue eating my food. Tonight, I'm feeling bold and brave.

"Sorry. You caught me off guard."

"I intend to keep you on your toes. This..." I point my fork at my food. "Is amazing."

"Thank you. What did you do today?"

"I went to secure my place as a winter fairy. Red glitter and fur could be my new thing."

"Visiting the castle may have to become part of my Christmas round too. I wonder if they need an elf."

"This park is big enough for the two of us. No need for you to hold my hand. Besides, Vinnie might sulk if I steal you away completely."

"I don't know. He seems very happy with the two blondes I sent him."

Raising an eyebrow, a smile widens on my face. "Here I was thinking karma dealt him some good luck."

"If he asks, that's what we'll tell him," he says mischievously, making me laugh.

Julian clears the plates, loading them into the dishwasher. He gets some ice cream out of the freezer, chops strawberries, and decorates them with mint. When he's done preparing the dessert, he places a martini glass loaded with ice cream in front of me.

"Did you make this?" I gesture to the vanilla ice cream.

"Sure. It's easy if you know how."

"I think I struck gold with you."

It tastes just as good as it looks. Julian smiles at my compliment. The ripe strawberries go down too easily, and it doesn't take me long to demolish the whole thing.

"I can only cook a few dishes. I'm not a chef or anything, but I do come with a theme park. I guess some girls would call me a catch."

"Don't forget the skateboarding trophies up in your room."

He laughs. "Maybe you're going to have to learn a trick or two to keep up with me."

"You love me just the way I am."

The words are out of my mouth before I can stop them. They hang in the air while I quickly clear the table. I load the dishwasher and turn it on. When I spin around, Julian catches me. My hand presses against his hard chest. His eyes search mine. I look away first and he captures my chin, cupping my face. Biting my lip, I stare into his beautiful eyes. I could look at him all day and still want more.

"The words I spoke last night... you heard them?"

I don't have to answer his question; he can read my face. He kisses my bottom lip, backing me up against the counter. My legs go around his waist and he perches me on the edge of the worktop.

"I love you, Kara. Just the way you are."

My insides fill with a sense of euphoria. Hearing him say those words clearly is even better than the first time. His face is raw with emotion. He's putting himself out there and asking me to catch him.

"I love you too, Julian."

That's all he needs to hear before he kisses me. I open to him, freely allowing him to take what he needs.

"Don't feel like you've got to say it."

"I wouldn't say it if I didn't feel it. For the first

time, I can see a future, rather than just a way to get by. You're everything I've ever wanted and more."

"There's no way I'm letting you go now."

He kisses me again while his hands explore my skin. The second I set eyes on Julian that day in the newspaper, I didn't know how special he was going to be. His perfect hair is trivial. His personality is his true beauty. He's more than a summer romance; he's more than I ever imagined possible.

"I'm ready to give you everything."

He stops kissing me to look into my eyes. "One day, I'm going to make you my wife."

Even though our life together has just begun, I would say yes in a heartbeat if he asked. I already belong to him. Call me young and foolish, but I know where my home is. It's right here with this man.

"I was talking about sex."

He laughs, rubbing his thumb against my swollen lips. "I know you were. I was just aiming for the sky."

"Trying to calm my nerves, you mean."

"Maybe."

I kiss him again, smiling against his lips. The idea of giving Julian everything feels right. Any doubts I had vanished the second I realised I'm in love with him. Julian means more than lust. It was always more. Abandoning the idea of a movie, we eagerly take our heat upstairs. We close the door to the rest of the world. It's just me and him, enjoying each other, and it's perfect.

CHAPTER FORTY SIX

BEAR

"Don't do that," my dad says, brushing me off.

"Just get in the chair. It's only until we reach the car park. Give the nurses this last little victory."

He stands and slowly moves to the wheelchair. I stay close to him in case he needs me but make no gesture to help.

"Fine. Are you happy now?" he bites out.

He sits down. I nod and place the overnight bag on his knee. The call came early this morning to say Dad can come home today. Instead of rushing, I got a coffee. I'm going to need the extra caffeine, especially when I know the office is the first place he will want to be.

"Why didn't you call Beatrice to pick you up?"

"She's already done enough. I don't want her to get the wrong idea about us."

"So, you're going to push her away again?" My frown knits into place.

He huffs instead of acknowledging my words. Pressing the button on the lift, we wait for its response. The silence my dad normally uses to brush me off will no longer work. This time, I let it slide, but only because I know he will come around.

Once in the car, he starts to relax. The leather seats and his familiar driver put his tension at ease and I can see him regaining his balance. He thinks he's in control.

"Would you like some help getting inside?" I ask when we stop at our house. He narrows his eyes at me as if I suggested committing a murder. After collecting his bag, I stay at his side but try to hide the fact I'm watching his every move.

My dad hovers near his office with a look of hope in his eyes. Voices coming from the kitchen shatter his plan. I can see him trying to work out which scenario will get him what he wants the quickest. After a groan, he abandons his initial thought and heads toward the kitchen. This time, I can't hide my smile.

Kara and Beatrice are preparing soup and warm bread rolls. When I catch Kara's gaze, her cheeks turn pink. Her smile is bright, and I can't resist stealing a kiss.

"Young love," Beatrice says, holding her hands to her chest.

"My new challenge in the park is to find a perfect match for everyone," Kara says.

My dad rolls his eyes while Beatrice shakes her head.

"I think you should concentrate on adding your female touches to this house. It could use some warmth," Beatrice replies.

"I'll be moving onto the university campus soon. My accommodation is already set up."

"You're welcome to stay here," Dad says.

"We'll be back at the weekends," I add.

"Wait, we never discussed you moving out." He can't hide the disbelief in his voice.

"Kara is staying in an all-girls dormitory. I don't want to miss the pillow fights and pyjama parties," I joke.

Kara chokes at my words and Beatrice pats her on the back.

"So, this is how it's going to be," Kara says, catching on quickly.

"Taking advantage of you while you're off guard is fun. Thanks for teaching me your mischievous ways."

"Don't forget I can get you back."

She raises her eyebrow, waiting for my reaction. Beatrice is watching us in fascination while my dad tries to eat his soup quickly. His welcome home party delays him from his work by about fifteen minutes. He's a workaholic, and not even a hospital scare is going to change that.

Once he retreats to his study, Kara and I move into the living room. Beatrice stays to clear the dishes.

"I like your dad. He's an older, grumpier version of you," Kara says.

"Hey, cheeky," I say, tackling Kara to the ground.

The sound of something breaking in the hallway stops us. Kara straightens her clothes as I roll off her. We both scramble to the door trying to spy on the situation. After signalling we need to be quiet, I slowly edge the door open.

Beatrice is on her knees picking up broken pottery. I'm about to offer to help her when my father hobbles into view.

"Leave the damn vase. It was ugly anyway."

"I'm sorry. I'm such a klutz. My jokes about remodelling your house didn't mean I wanted to destroy your antiques."

"A woman's touch is what this place needs. I don't disagree." He bends down to help her pick up the last few pieces.

"Ouch," Beatrice says, shaking her finger.

My dad takes her hand and looks at the wound. "You should've left it like I asked."

"Pipe down. It's only a scratch."

"You're bleeding on my carpet."

"Give me my hand back and I'll clean it up." He lowers his head to her finger. She pulls her hand back like it's caught on fire.

"Did you just kiss my cut?" she says in shock.

"What if I did?"

"We're not five." Beatrice is usually a pussycat and it's nice to see her stand up for herself for once.

"Trust me, I know. It's going to take me way too long to get up off the floor." His voice softens.

"You're hopeless. Come on."

She pulls him up and they slowly make their way to the kitchen.

"I think your dad secretly likes Beatrice more than he lets on," Kara says.

"They do this crazy dance all the time."

"Maybe he needs a little nudge."

"If my dad catches you meddling in his life, he'll think he has a free pass to return the favour. You'll be enrolling yourself onto God knows what course."

"Beatrice won't turn out to be an evil stepmother. She's kind and loving, they're good qualities. I'd have her as a surrogate mother," Kara says.

"Beatrice wouldn't hurt a fly. I wouldn't be against them dating."

Kara has a look of mischief on her face. I tickle her again and we break out into laughter as she fights me for control. I'm about to kiss her when Beatrice enters the living room.

"What are you two doing on the floor?"

Kara points at me for an explanation. No words come out of my mouth, so instead, I chase her up the stairs.

"See, it's already starting," Kara says.

"What's starting?"

"Beatrice's stepmother duties."

"If you've got fairy-tale fantasies, the park is the place to be. I might be able to help you out with a few prince charming ones too," I say with a wink.

"Okay. I'll drop it."

The sparkle in her eye tells me she doesn't mean what she says. Having Kara around is going to make things more colourful. The way I easily fell in love with her was something I didn't expect to happen. Watching her win over my dad is going to be interesting. Kara is already getting under his skin and I don't want to miss a thing.

CHAPTER FORTY SEVEN

KARA

THREE MONTHS LATER

The first snowflake falls as I anxiously stare out the window. I can't believe my sister is having a December wedding. It wouldn't be so bad if she hadn't chosen a picturesque village in North Yorkshire. It's a beautiful barn conversion in the middle of nowhere. Thick snow and log cabins should be the perfect scene, but when I'm over two hours away, it's not so impressive.

Toby elbows me to bring my attention back to the lecturer. I have a couple of classes before we'll be on our way. The thought of skipping is running through my mind, however, in typical Kara style, I've already got off to a bad start with my mentor. Being late on the first day is a sin. Being late and falling down the stairs makes me a definite sinner in Catherine's eyes.

She has me down as a troublemaker. I had a big bruise on my knee for weeks. Even the hobble in my step didn't soften her glare. My first day jitters strike again.

I've been trying my hardest to change her mind about me. I hoped she'd cut me some slack with it being the beginning of term, but as she pointed out, I was the only one who was late. Skipping class isn't a good idea, even if I have a valid excuse.

Looking at the projector, I realise I'm behind. I haven't taken more than half a page of notes. Luckily, Toby is scribbling like crazy on his notepad. I take a sip of my water, trying to focus on the class. The snowflakes outside are getting bigger and faster. I slip my phone out of my pocket to find a message from Julian.

Stop thinking about the snow. It's fine.

He knows me so well. My smile is instant, although it gains me an eye roll from Toby.

Why? Do you have a snow plough hidden away in your garage?

The park has a few, but they won't get you far. Besides, it's just a few flakes. It's not settling.

I can't see the ground from the third floor, and

he knows it. I'll have to trust he isn't just trying to calm my nerves. Sitting back in my chair, I try to relax.

"Once you've written down the notes, we're done for the morning. I'll see you back here in one hour," Catherine says.

The room breaks out into chatter as people begin to leave. I turn to Toby, placing my hand on his arm. "If you sit in the back, maybe she won't notice I'm missing."

He narrows his eyes at me. "We always sit here. It's a stupid plan, besides, you're not leaving me behind. I may not be your plus one, but I'm not missing your sister's wedding. Now, let's go get a sandwich. I'm starving."

The cold air instantly gives me chills as we step outside. I pull my scarf tightly around my neck. The wet ground doesn't look so bad and the snow is creating dirty sludge. Choosing a cheese sandwich from the deli, I guide Toby towards the library.

"Where're we going?"

"I need to use the photocopier."

"What you mean is you didn't take any notes and you need mine."

I pout and he rolls his eyes as he follows me into the revolving door. "Sorry. I'm just anxious to get out of here."

"The two weeks off will do you good. I think you're burned out," he says with concern.

"You're right. Once we get to the cabin, I'll feel better."

"Stop dreaming of hot tub and romantic walks with Julian," he teases.

"You're just jealous." I laugh.

"I'm not ready to settle down."

"When Sophie returns from Europe, you'll change your mind."

He doesn't look convinced but I know Toby. He misses her, even if he hasn't said anything. Sophie is in Spain, spending the holidays with her grandparents and Toby's been sulking since she left.

Placing my card into the reader, I put Toby's notepad in the copier. When the sheet comes out, I groan at Toby's childish doodle of the male anatomy.

"It's okay. I can turn it into a flower."

He laughs. "Only you would say that."

"I'd die if someone thought I drew that. If Catherine saw it, she'd probably give me an extra assignment."

"You could scribble it out. I drew it in pencil, so it'll easily come off mine."

Using a marker, I turn it into a flower and add some colour. Toby takes a picture of it.

"You didn't just send that to Julian?"

His smirk confirms my suspicion. My boys are always conspiring against me, but I'm just happy to see them get along.

The second half of the day passes quickly. The

snow stays away, and I practically dance when classes are finally over. I gather my bags then head for the door. Julian is waiting outside with a warm drink and a muffin. I kiss him on the lips before taking my treats. The smell of cinnamon makes my mouth water.

"You shouldn't have," Toby says, stealing my muffin and taking a bite.

I'm about to curse when Julian hands me a second muffin, which earns him another kiss.

After collecting our luggage, we board the train right on schedule. Winter break has officially begun. I sit with Julian while Toby disappears down the carriage.

"I can't wait to get you all to myself," he says, kissing my hand.

"We were together last weekend." I point out.

"Yes, but this is different. It's me, you, and a log cabin."

His grin is laced with mischief. I can imagine it now. It'll be just us in the hot tub with a glass of bubbly.

"I like the sound of that."

I lean over and kiss him softly on his warm lips. Hungry for more, he nibbles at my mouth. It turns into a hot lip-locking session until Toby coughs, signalling he's back. I smooth down my hair, trying to hide my blush. It's so easy to become lost in Julian.

A text from my sister bursts any lustful thoughts.

SOS

What's wrong?

I don't think I can do this.

This day can't end quickly enough. I know my sister loves Derrick. Whatever her problem is, we can solve it together. I need to call her, but it's better to let her calm down first. Snuggling into Julian's shoulder, I take comfort in him. His closeness settles my worries and I feel more prepared to deal with Helen. Something tells me this break isn't going to be the romantic getaway Julian is hoping for.

CHAPTER

FORTY EIGHT

KARA

The train is almost empty when it arrives at the station. The announcement jolts me from my seat. I'm almost certain I snored a little on the journey. Toby laughs at my confusion as I lock eyes with him. Luckily, Julian doesn't seem to notice my startled gaze. After dragging my luggage off the train, I see Hayley and Anna waiting for us on the platform.

"Where's your mum?"

"She said she needed a break, so we came with Beatrice to pick you up," Anna says.

Beatrice appears from the ticket office, holding a tourist guide book. Her hiking boots and thick winter coat fit perfectly with the scenery. The rest of us look like we've forgotten that summer is over in comparison.

"Please tell me the guide book isn't to find the barn," I say.

"It's for after the wedding. I plan to spend a few days exploring the area. This guide is going to make sure I don't miss a thing."

The car park is icy, and I hold onto Julian's arm to steady myself. Beatrice leads us to an old blue minivan which we all climb inside. I want to ask the girls about the wedding, but I have a bad feeling about everything. Their chatter is full of excitement. There's no indication of anything being wrong, and nobody mentions Helen's meltdown. I tried calling her a few times on the way but had no luck. When the venue comes into view, Derrick is pacing on the deck, talking on the phone.

I follow Julian into our log cabin, placing my bag on the bed. He pulls me into a kiss and I almost forget I need to find Helen. I rest my forehead against his. It's been a few days since we've had time alone, but the wedding is more important.

"I'm sorry. As much as I want to ravish you, I need to go find my sister. She's having a crisis."

He kisses my forehead, rubbing his hands down my arms. Our fingertips hook and I indulge in a few more pecks on his lips before we break apart.

"I'll be as quick as I can."

Once outside, I pull my scarf back into place, checking nobody's watching me. I want to see Helen alone so we can talk freely; I don't want to panic anyone with her wedding jitters. Derrick's lost in his conversation on the phone, and Beatrice is unloading food bags from the minivan. Hayley and Anna are nowhere in sight. I take my phone out of my pocket and go behind the cabins to call my sister. Instead of answering the phone, she sends me a message saying she's in the barn. I glance around one last time before slipping inside.

Helen's sitting at a small round table, nervously tapping her foot against the floor. A large glass of wine rocks between her fingers.

"What's wrong?" I ask softly.

"The question is what's right? My cake hasn't arrived, my veil has lost some pearls, and the photographer has got a stomach bug. It's a sign I shouldn't be doing this. Our relationship has already hit the rocks once before," she says in a high-pitched voice like she's having a panic attack.

"It's not a sign. Calm down. We can work this out. Beatrice can mend the veil. Let's start with that."

I message Beatrice, asking her to go to the village to find some pearls or jewels. Helen runs her hand through her hair. The tapping rhythm of her foot slows its pace.

"You're right. I need to calm down and think this through."

"When's the cake supposed to be arriving?"

"I don't know. I've lost the number of the bakery."

"We can find it on the internet. All we need is a few clues."

Sitting together, we work our way through Helen's social media. Eventually, we find the bakery and she calls them while I try to solve the last problem. I don't know anyone with a professional camera, never mind someone willing to travel all this way.

Beatrice slips inside the barn, waving her supplies. I pass her the veil and she immediately gets to work on it. After a few curses from burning her fingers on the glue gun, she holds up the veil for Helen to see. For the first time since I got here, Helen smiles.

"The cake has been delivered to a church down the road. The bakery is going to call me back when the delivery man has it back safe in the van."

Crossing my fingers, I hold them up in the air.

She hugs me tightly. "I knew you'd come through for me."

My sister and I can work anything out if we put our minds together.

"I hardly did anything. You did all this on your own."

"I needed you," she says, squeezing my shoulder. I love my sister and want her to have the perfect day.

"If we can't find a photographer, everyone will take pictures on their phones."

She offers a weak smile.

Helen is cheery by the time I leave her with the twins. They're having a midnight feast to celebrate. I find Julian in our log cabin, making grilled cheese toasties.

"It's time we check out the hot tub," I say.

"That's the best news of the day. Did you manage to sort everything with Helen?"

"We're missing a photographer, but everything else is back on track. Everyone will take pictures on the day. It's not the worst thing that could've happened."

Once I'm bikini ready, I slip into the warm water next to Julian. He hands me a glass of bubbly, and for the first time today, I allow myself to relax.

"Tomorrow can't come soon enough," I say.

"We should have a spontaneous Las Vegas wedding. No planning. We'll just go."

"The day after graduation, if you still want me, it's a deal."

"As if I could live without you."

He pulls me into a kiss. We may have only been together for a few months, but this feels right. Julian is my soulmate. The only man for me. Fate gave me my perfect match and I'm never letting go.

"Tell me more about this photo business."

"The photographer has a stomach bug or something and can't make it."

"Have you tried to find a replacement?"

"This close to Christmas in the middle of the countryside, I doubt we'd have any takers."

"As much as this pains me to say, I think our

romantic night is going to have to be cut short. Maybe I can pull some strings and find your sister what she needs."

Julian leaves me in the hot tub with a beautiful view, but not the one I want. My sister already loves him, but if he can pull this off, maybe she will forgive us for eloping to get married.

———

Toby is watching television when I enter his cabin. He hands me the bowl of treats when I sit next to him on the sofa. His eyes never wander from the true crime show he's watching.

"What happened to your romantic plans with Julian?"

"He's on wedding duties." I put a piece of popping candy onto my tongue and let it crackle.

"There's no way I could be as good as him," he says truthfully.

"Even I gave up trying for that trophy."

I helped Helen when I could, but only Julian can perform miracles.

"All hail King Julian."

I swat him with the pillow, and he goes straight on the defensive. "Don't be jealous. You've got some good qualities too."

"Oh, yeah? Like what?"

"Well, if you can't think of any, I'm struggling too."

He grabs his pillow and hits me on the shoulder. Feathers begin to fly everywhere as we attack each other. Julian may be my perfect match, but Toby will always be my best friend.

That night, I fall asleep snuggled up to Julian. I cross my fingers for a smoothly running day tomorrow. I don't know if Julian's attempts were successful, but I have faith.

CHAPTER FORTY NINE

BEAR

They say beauty is in the eye of the beholder. The bride is beautiful, don't get me wrong. Helen and Derrick look great together, but it's Kara who has my attention. She looks radiant in her bridesmaid dress and I can't take my eyes off her. The smile she saves just for me is giving me tingles right down to the core. She's breath-taking and completely mine. Watching her tuck her hair behind her ear with a smile on her face is enough for me to know I'm a lucky guy. If I hadn't come home this summer, I might have missed my opportunity to find my happily ever after. My dad was right; the park is the key to my future and I'm no longer afraid to embrace it.

It took me most of the night to find my girl what she needs. Lance is a local retired photographer and an old friend of Dad's. For once, my connections got the right attention. As soon as I told him who I was, he took down the details. First thing this morning, he arrived with a van full of equipment.

The registrar clears her throat, signalling she is about to start the ceremony. Kara takes her seat next to her nieces. Derrick lets out the breath he's almost suffocating on and everyone laughs. The tension in his shoulders relaxes as he whispers words to his bride. She smiles and kisses his cheek.

At the beginning of the summer, I never imagined I would want a partnership like that, someone to take away my worries. Now I realise having someone special makes everything a little easier.

The words begin to spill from the registrar, and the couple say their vows. A victorious cheer echoes around the barn as they kiss. Hayley and Anna pretend to cover their eyes. The smile on my face is pure happiness. This is my family now and I love every one of them. Weddings are a way of bringing people together, and I'm appreciating everything and everyone in this room.

After signing the marriage papers and posing for a few pictures, the music begins to play. *Canon* by Pachelbel is a song I'm familiar with. Classical music is usually playing when I attend something I don't want to be at. Kara has even changed my views on those events too.

I rise from my seat with everyone else to watch the newlyweds exit the room. As I turn, my eyes latch onto the last person I expected to see. Hovering at the back in his pristine royal blue suit is my father.

Toby nudges me. "Isn't that your dad standing in the far corner?"

"Yeah." I smile happy to see him here.

"I thought he couldn't make it."

"That's what he said. I'm guessing he had a change of heart. Beatrice probably has something to do with it."

"She is a persuasive woman."

Toby gestures to the suit he has on and I smirk. He thought he would get away with trousers and a shirt. Beatrice quickly marched him down to the local charity shop. When he met me in the pub later that day, he even had new shoes.

Taking a glass of Bucks Fizz, I join my dad by the fireplace. It's been over a week since I've seen him because I've busy at university. Looking into the fire, I mirror his stance by leaning my glass against the wooden plinth.

"You know people are going to start thinking you've gone soft in your old age." I tease him.

A whisper of a smile crosses his lips. "How could I deny Beatrice a dancing partner when she's done so much for me?"

Every single person here would welcome a dance

with the lady in question. I don't tell him that though. It's nice to see him doing something which doesn't involve work. If allowing him to think he's doing a good deed makes him feel better... then I think Beatrice won this round.

Toby joins us with his beer. "I need to watch some sports to take the edge off," he jokes.

"I'm sure you'll find some rugby or football if you look hard enough," I reply.

He adjusts his tie, loosening it from his neck. Someone shouts my name and I follow the voice. Stepping outside, the white snow blankets the view. Kara holds her hand out to me and I wrap myself around her shoulders.

"You're cold."

"It's only for a few more photos."

The photographer takes a couple more pictures and the rest of the day passes quickly. It isn't long before I have Kara up on the dance floor. The twins have Toby spinning them around like ballerinas. My dad stays true to his word and has Beatrice in his arms as they move to the music. The newlyweds are sharing their first few dances together. As I look around, I realise how lucky I am, and not just because I have Kara.

"Let's step out onto the balcony for a minute," I whisper.

Her eyes lift to meet mine and she kisses me

softly. We head outside and I secretly hope nobody notices. It'll be nice to have her to myself for a while.

"You look beautiful today." I pull her closer to me.

"You're quite handsome yourself." She touches the flower on my suit.

"Stop. You'll make me blush." Her smile lights up her whole face.

"How's the skateboarding prize coming along for the charity auction?"

I run my finger along the edge of her shoulder strap. Her skin feels soft. "Let's not talk about that tonight. We can worry about everything else later. I want to enjoy you and me."

"Are you getting all sentimental on me?" she says with a coy smile.

"Maybe I am."

"I love you." She holds eye contact.

"I love you forever."

Pulling her into a gentle kiss leaves me hungry for more. Her hair looks too pretty tonight for me to touch it. Instead, I run my fingers along her collarbone.

Laughter breaks my trance. The patio doors close loudly as someone approaches the balcony. Kara pulls me deeper into the shadows as we continue to lose ourselves in each other.

"I can't wait to have you all to myself," I say.

"Me too, but for now, we should get back inside."

I fireman's lift her over my shoulder. She laughs,

pretending to struggle. I stop in my tracks when I see who has come outside. Slowly, I place Kara back on the ground. She's about to ask me what's wrong, when she sees my dad and Beatrice kissing.

"Maybe Christmas wishes do come true." Kara giggles, pushing me through the door.

CHAPTER FIFTY

KARA

Snow crunches under my feet as we walk across the open meadow. Beatrice's warm winter coat is snug over my woolly jumper. My family is at the airport, dreaming of sun, sea, and sandy beaches. I'm happy to be here, in North Yorkshire, with my amazing boyfriend. I grab for Julian's hand as I stumble through the deep snow. He pulls me close, steadying my steps.

"We're almost there," Julian says.

"You're being all secretive."

"I'm taking full advantage of having you to myself."

"I like the sound of that."

Leaning in, I expect a kiss. However, Julian has a different idea. He spins me around, covering my eyes with his thick blue gloves. He leads me a little farther before stopping. He keeps me in suspense for a few more seconds as his lips lower to my ear.

"I want to make you feel as special as you make me feel. This is a small token to show you how much I care. I hope you like it."

Glass crystals and fairy lights enhance what is already a picturesque view. The beautiful English countryside stretches for miles. Snow covers every surface like a soft blanket. Two deck chairs and a picnic basket are laid out before me.

"This is perfect."

I take a seat, watching Julian prepare two travel mugs of hot chocolate. He adds cream, marshmallows, and candy sticks before passing me the sugary treat.

"Who would've guessed the girl who pushed me in the lake would be the one to be sitting here with me right now?"

"I was showing you the bigger picture. That lake has more potential than you realised."

"When I saw you in my theme park, I knew I was in trouble."

"Some things are meant to be. When I first saw your picture in the newspaper, I thought you were something I'd like to take a closer look at."

"Oh, so now the truth comes out. You're a gold digger, after my money." He teases.

I laugh. "I didn't know who you were at the time. I thought you were some model they'd brought in to make the theme park look desirable. When I met you at the youth centre, I had no idea how special you were. Now I know you're the grump that scares the visitors away from Blue Oaks."

"You're hilarious. I *made* this summer for you."

"I can't disagree."

He places both our cups down onto the snow. Pulling me out of the chair, he spins me around until we both fall over, laughing.

"I'm going to make every season amazing for you."

His kisses are sweet. Brushing the snow from my trousers, I help Julian back to his feet.

"Next summer, I'm going to give the swan ride a romance on the lake makeover."

"Good idea. Hopefully, fewer people will end in the lake that way. We should ban mobile phones too. That way they'll have to talk to each other. Getting some duck food in the shape of heart confetti will add the final touch."

"Are you making fun of my idea?"

"No. It'll be a huge success for Valentine's Day, but the boys might have something to say about it being so girly though."

"I can add spider webs for the boys."

"Hearts and spider webs. What a combination."

"It's a work in progress. I have a year to think about it."

"Nope, Valentine's is two months away. Your application is successful. I'm putting you in charge."

"Don't you worry. I have this. I accept your challenge."

I've no clue where to start with my new mission. One thing I do know is my friends Lynne, Beatrice, and Vinnie will help.

The view up here is beautiful. Julian takes my hand, ready to set off back to the cabin. I pull him around to face me. I'll never get enough of this man. I lean in to kiss him one last time. My arms rest on his chest, his cold nose lightly touches mine, and my foot pops up. *Perfection.*

"I love you."

"I love you too."

Who knows what the future holds? The only thing I do know is I want to spend it with Julian.

The End.

ACKNOWLEDGMENTS

When I finish reading a book, the first thing I do is read the acknowledgements. I use it as a cool down to ease me away from the story. I'm telling you this because I'm feeling the pressure to get this section right.

I've wanted to write a book I could be proud of for many years. My journey started with an idea and blossomed through friendship.

After reading *Reasonable Doubts* by Kyra Lennon, I knew I wanted to work with her to edit my book. Her words bring her stories to life and it was important to me to find someone who had written books I liked. Thank you Karen Sanders Editing for everything you have done for me and more.

Thank you to my savvy betas Annamarie, Carmen, Diane, Jennifer, Karen, Kaye, Lucy, Melanie, Mich,

Molly, Rebecca, Ruth and Tracy. Your advice and input has helped shape this story to w nat it is today.

Thank you to authors Sandra Seymour and Kyra Lennon for your writing coach services, and Mich Feeney for proofreading.

Kate McMurry, author of Girl Vs Ghost, I owe you a big thank you for your advice on reading before jumping in. Understanding the concept was just as important as finding the words.

Thank you to Melissa and Sarah. Although the story you read is nothing like the book I published, you both helped with my confidence.

Thank you to everyone who helped me with this project. Big or small, it means the world to me.

ABOUT THE AUTHOR

Danielle lives in Yorkshire, England, with her husband, daughter, and tortoise. She enjoys reading, long walks, and crafting. Her dreams include writing stories, visiting magical places, and staying young at heart. The people who know her describe her as someone who has her head in the clouds and her mind in a book.

Thank you for taking the time to read my story. If you enjoyed it, please consider writing a short review.

Printed in Great Britain
by Amazon